NIGHT OF THE HOMEWORK ZOMBIES

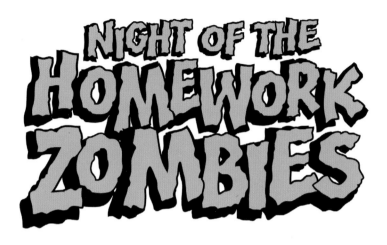

Librarian Reviewer
Laurie K. Holland
Media Specialist (National Board Certified), Edina, MN
MA in Elementary Education, Minnesota State University, Mankato, MN

Reading Consultant
Elizabeth Stedem
Educator/Consultant, Colorado Springs, CO
MA in Elementary Education, University of Denver, CO

Graphic Sparks are published by Stone Arch Books,
151 Good Counsel Drive, P.O. Box 669,
Mankato, Minnesota 56002.
www.stonearchbooks.com

Library of Congress Cataloging-in-Publication Data
Nickel, Scott.
    Night of the Homework Zombies / by Scott Nickel; illustrated by Steve Harpster.
    p. cm. — (Graphic Sparks)
    ISBN-13: 978-1-59889-035-8 (hardcover)
    ISBN-10: 1-59889-035-2 (hardcover)
    ISBN-13: 978-1-59889-172-0 (paperback)
    ISBN-10: 1-59889-172-3 (paperback)
    1. Graphic novels. I. Harpster, Steve. II. Title. III. Series.
PN6727.N544N54 2005
741.5—dc22   2005026687

Summary: Mr. Winklepoof, the new substitute teacher, is really a mad scientist. His
goal: turn every kid in school into a brain-boggled zombie who loves homework! "Study!
Study!" they chant. Only Trevor knows the truth. And only Trevor can save his friends, and
himself, from this truly horrible fate!

Art Director: Heather Kindseth
Production Manager: Sharon Reid
Production/Design: James Liebman, Mie Tsuchida
Production Assistance: Bob Horvath, Eric Murray

1 2 3 4 5 6 11 10 09 08 07 06

Printed in the United States of America.

NIGHT OF THE
HOMEWORK
ZOMBIES

BY SCOTT NICKEL

ILLUSTRATED BY STEVE HARPSTER

STONE ARCH BOOKS
Minneapolis San Diego

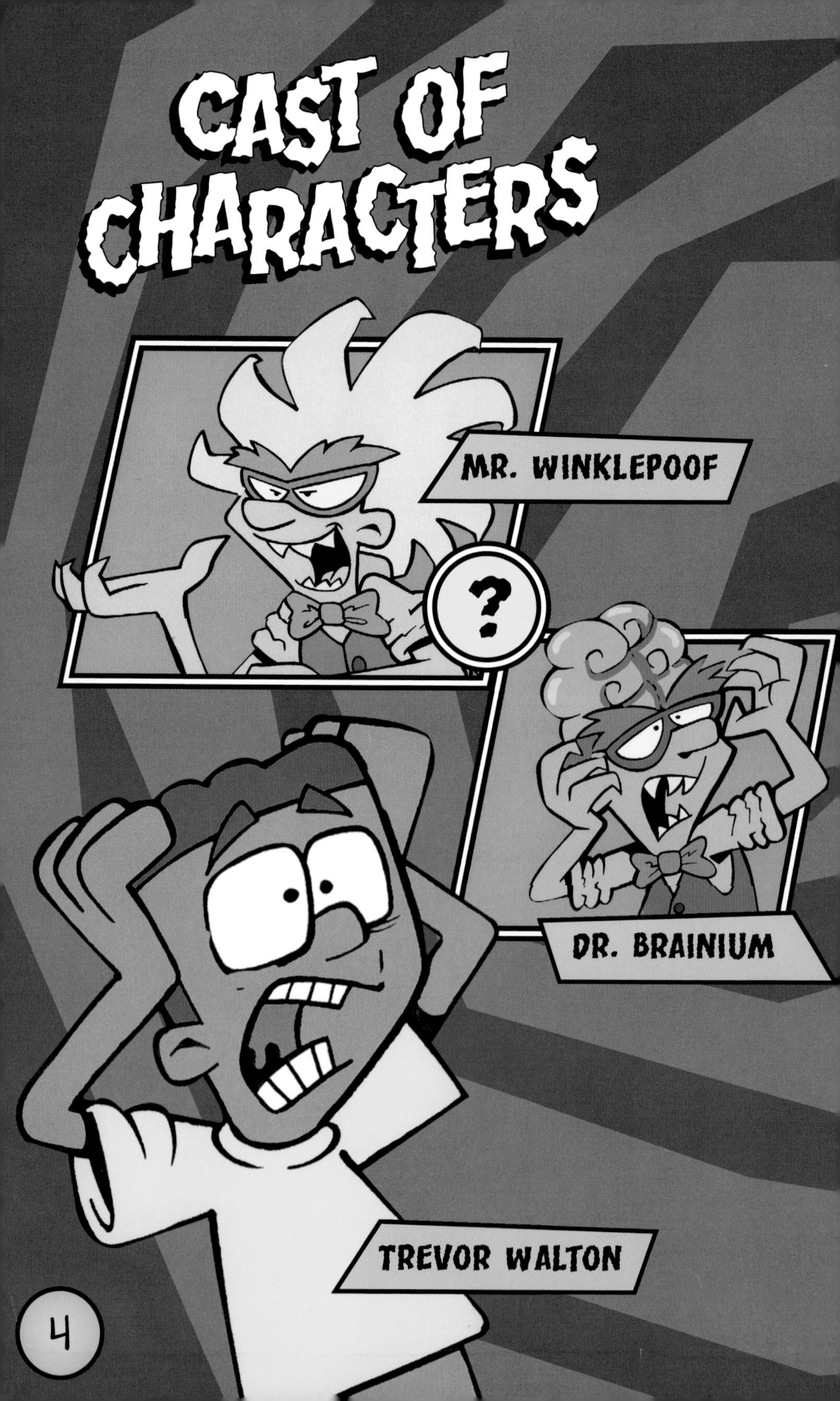
CAST OF CHARACTERS
MR. WINKLEPOOF
?
DR. BRAINIUM
TREVOR WALTON

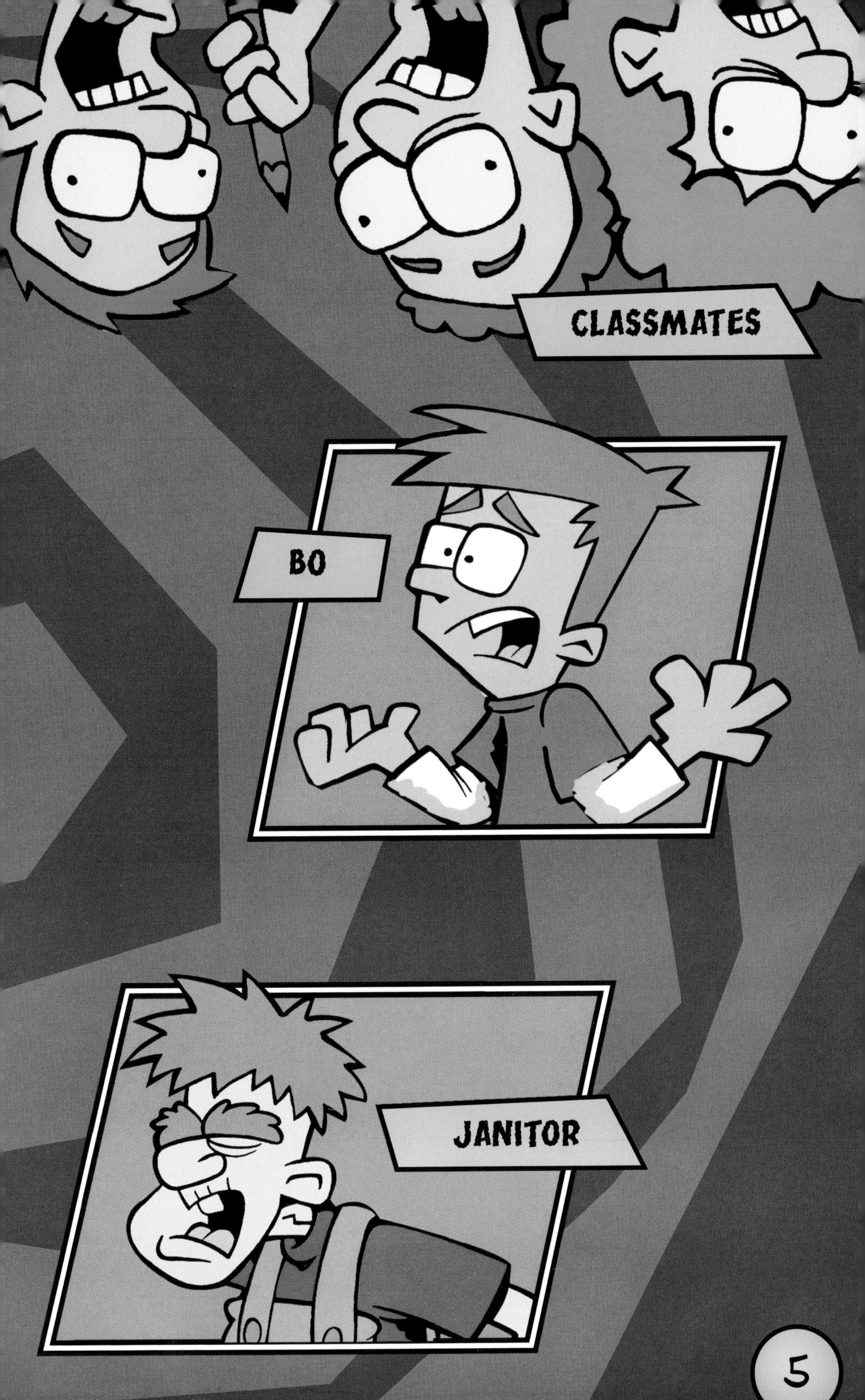
CLASSMATES
BO
JANITOR

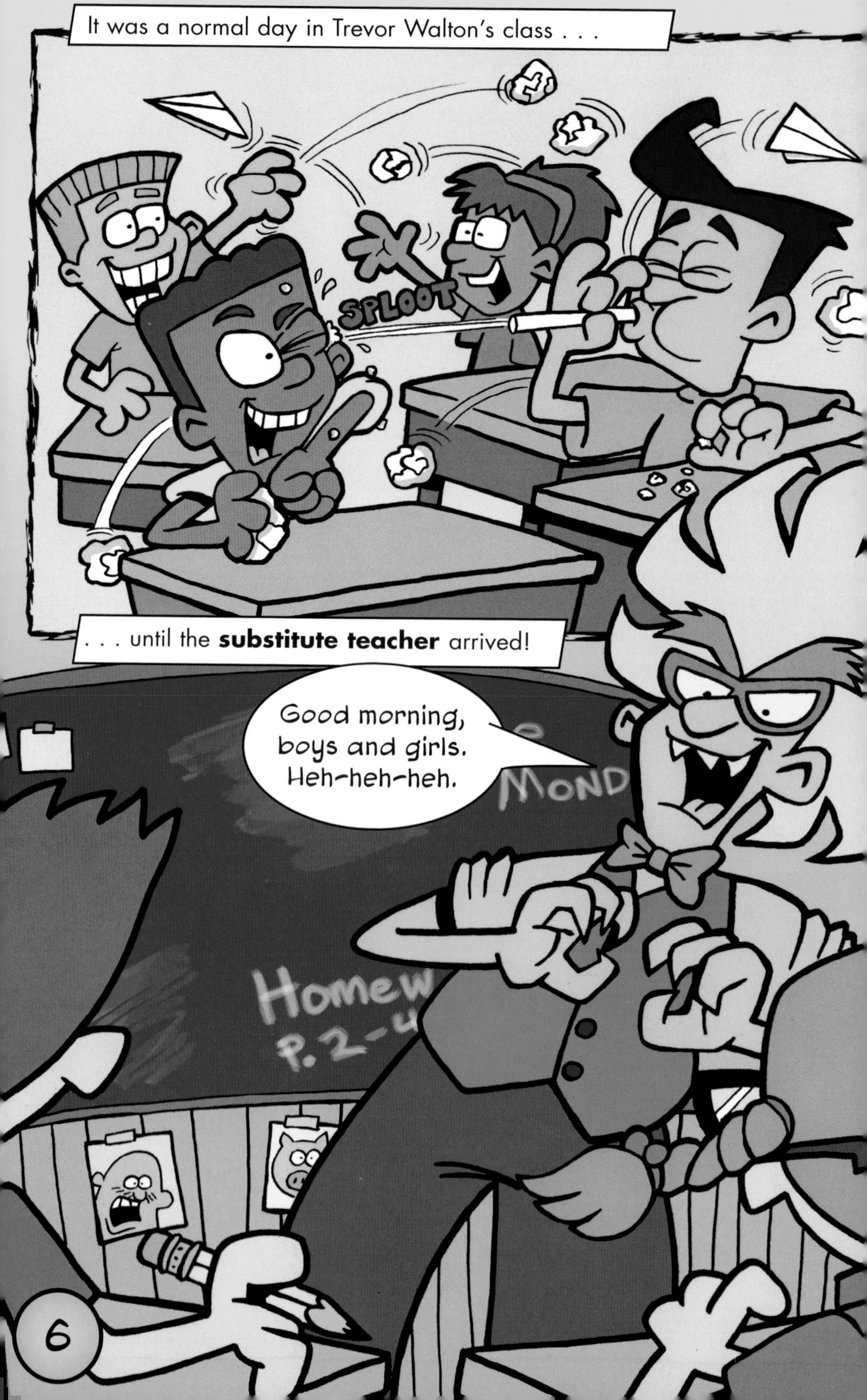
It was a normal day in Trevor Walton's class . . .
SPLOOT
. . . until the **substitute teacher** arrived!
Good morning, boys and girls. Heh-heh-heh.

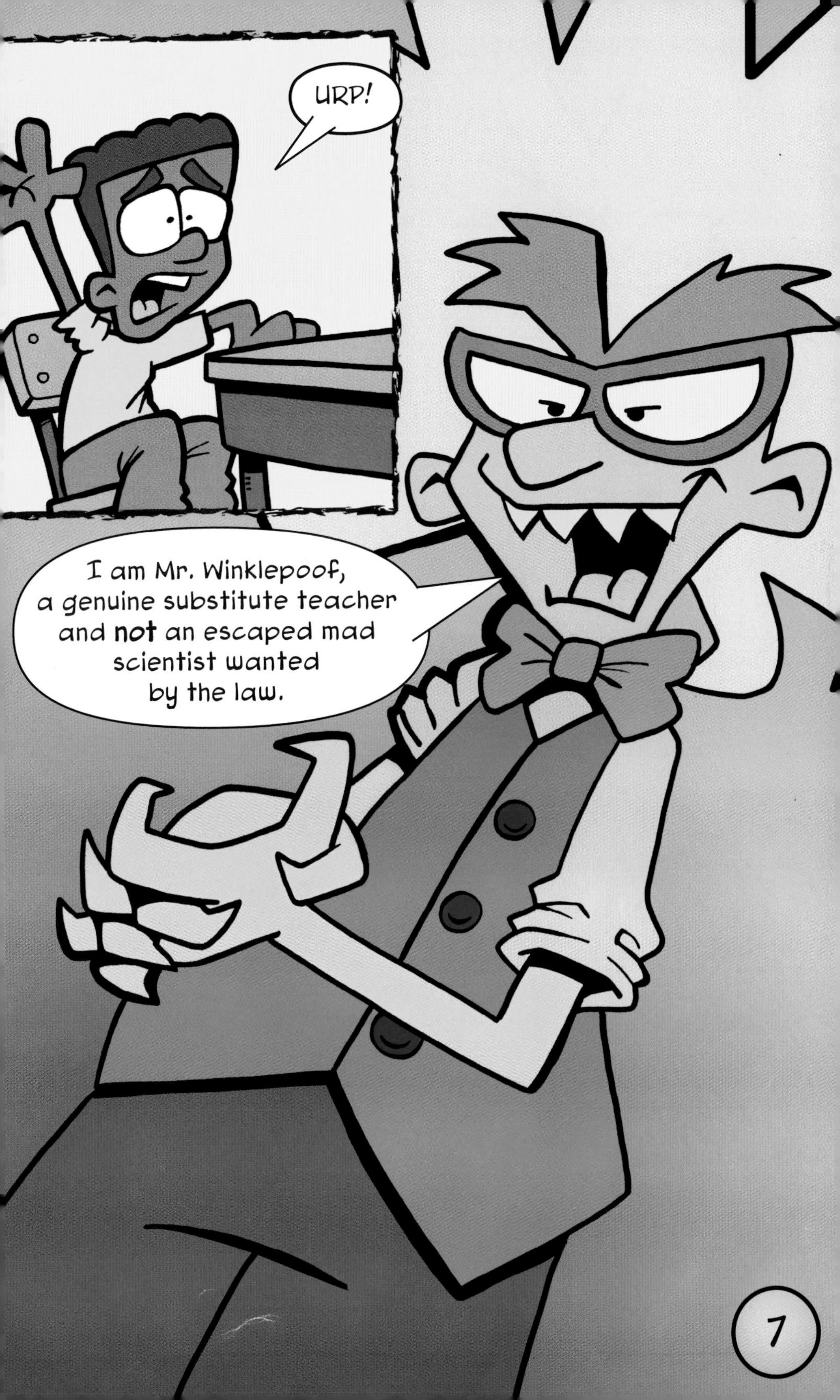
URP!
I am Mr. Winklepoof, a genuine substitute teacher and **not** an escaped mad scientist wanted by the law.

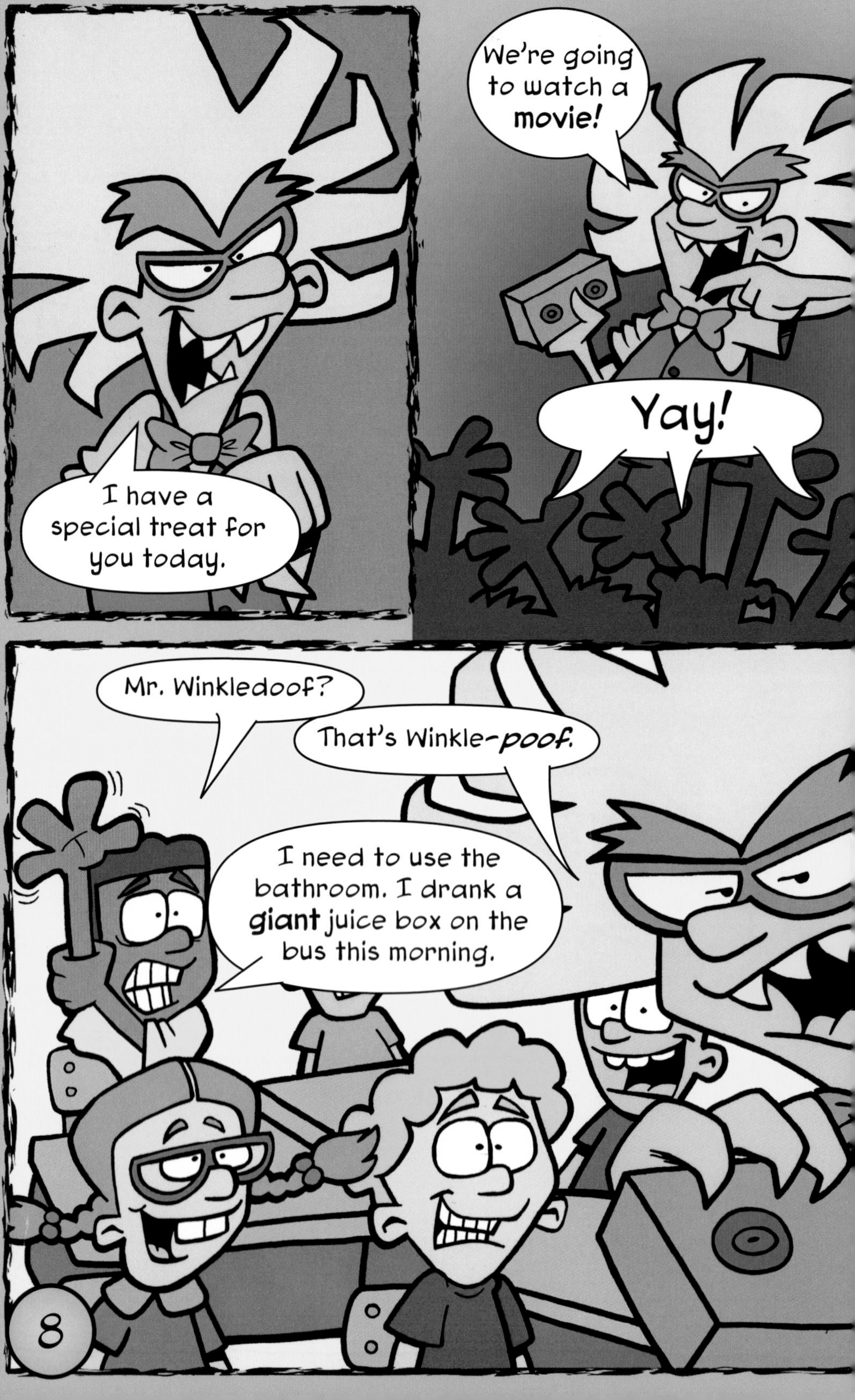
I have a special treat for you today.
We're going to watch a movie!
Yay!
Mr. Winkledoof?
That's Winkle-poof.
I need to use the bathroom. I drank a giant juice box on the bus this morning.

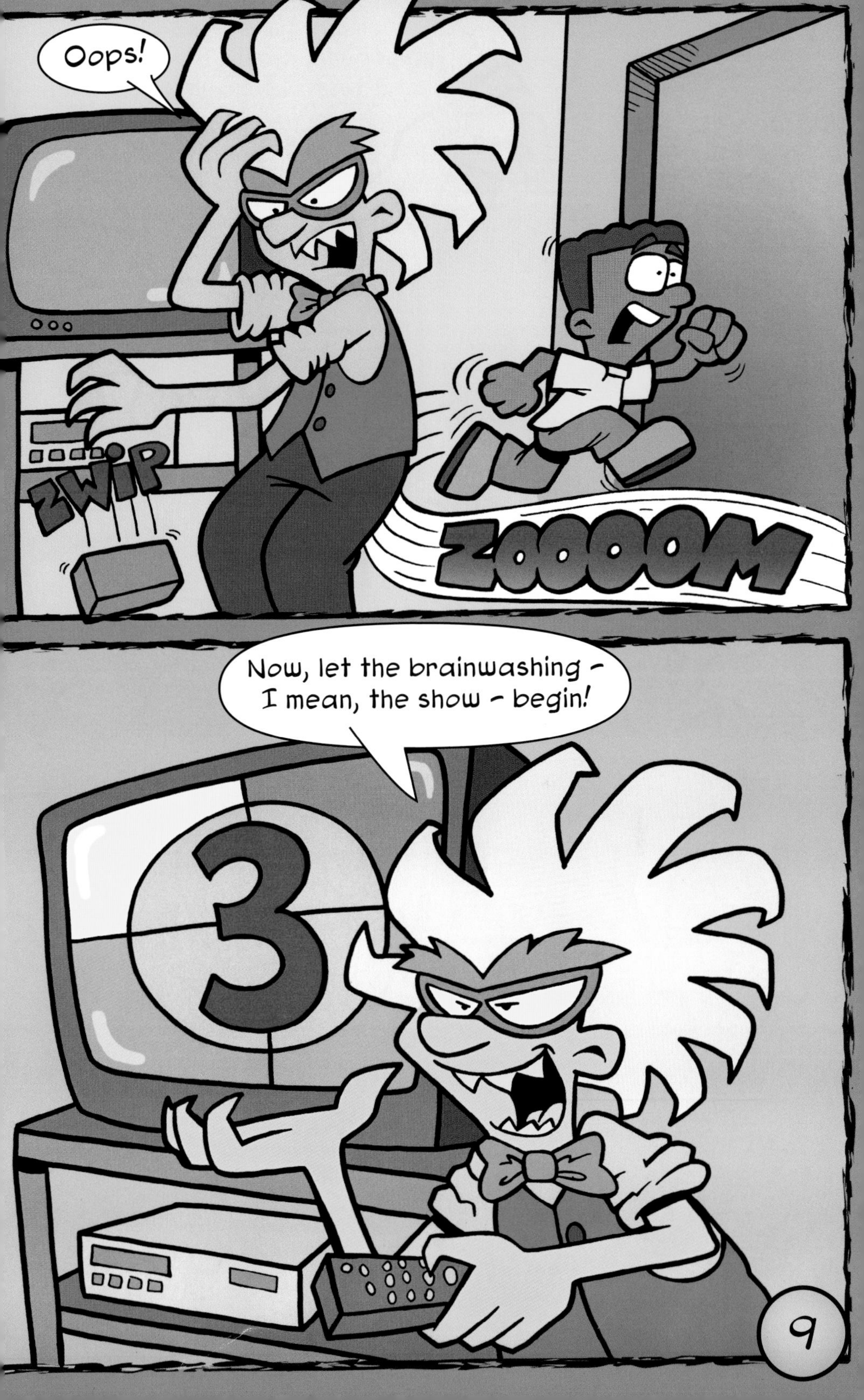
Oops!
ZWIP
ZOOOOM
Now, let the brainwashing -
I mean, the show - begin!
3

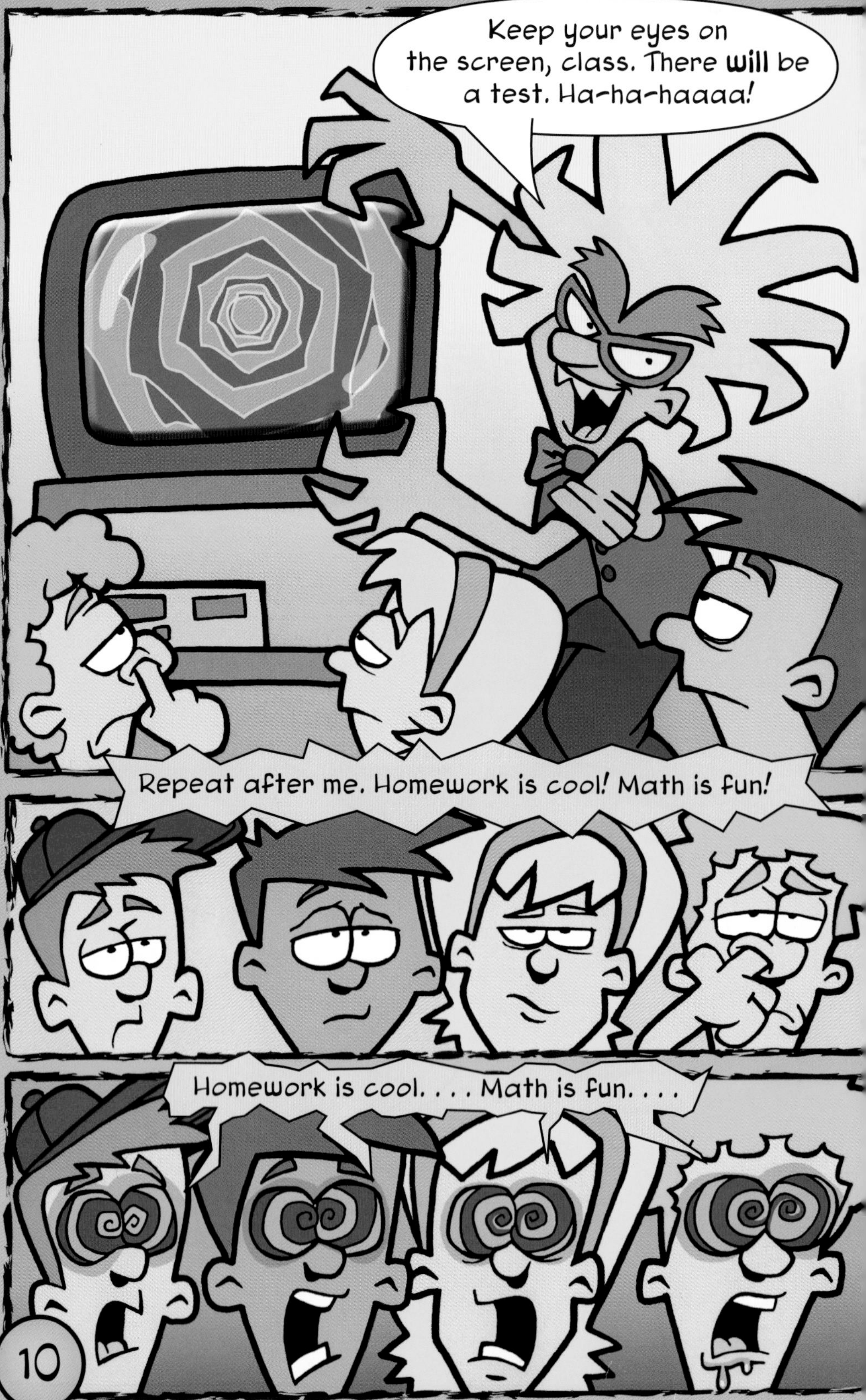
Keep your eyes on the screen, class. There **will** be a test. Ha-ha-haaaa!
Repeat after me. Homework is cool! Math is fun!
Homework is cool. . . . Math is fun. . . .

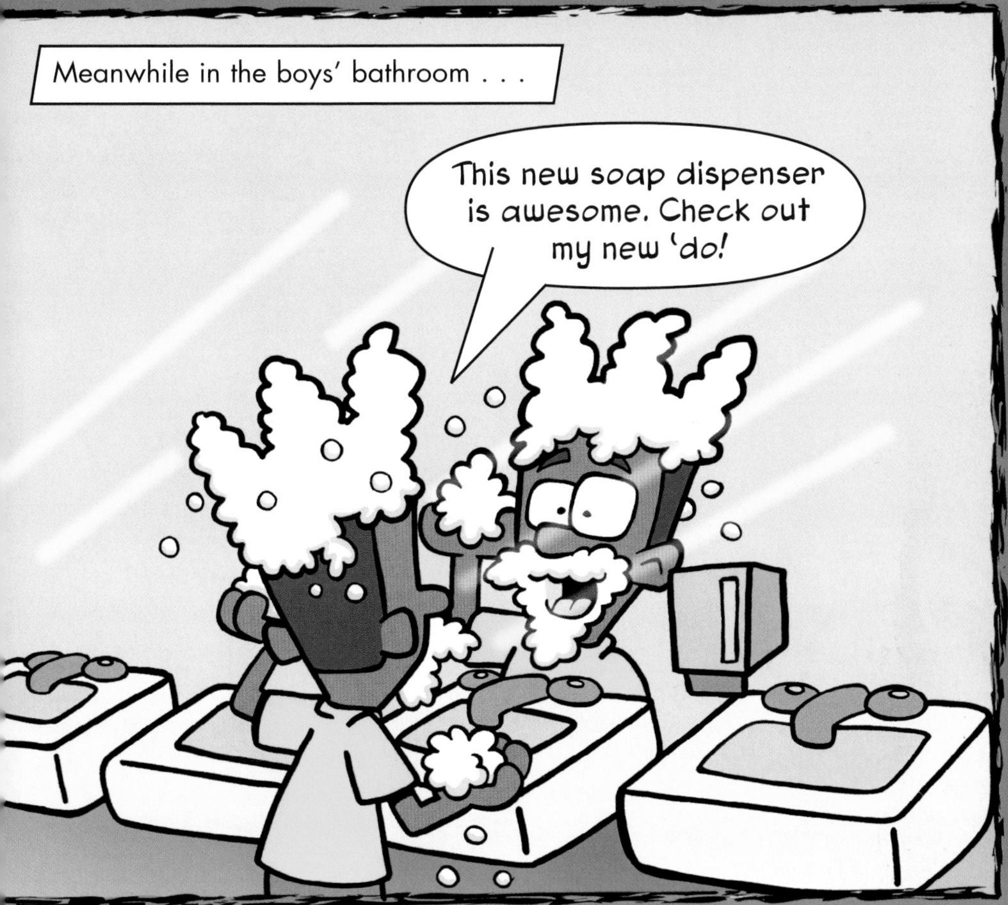
Meanwhile in the boys' bathroom . . .
This new soap dispenser is awesome. Check out my new 'do!

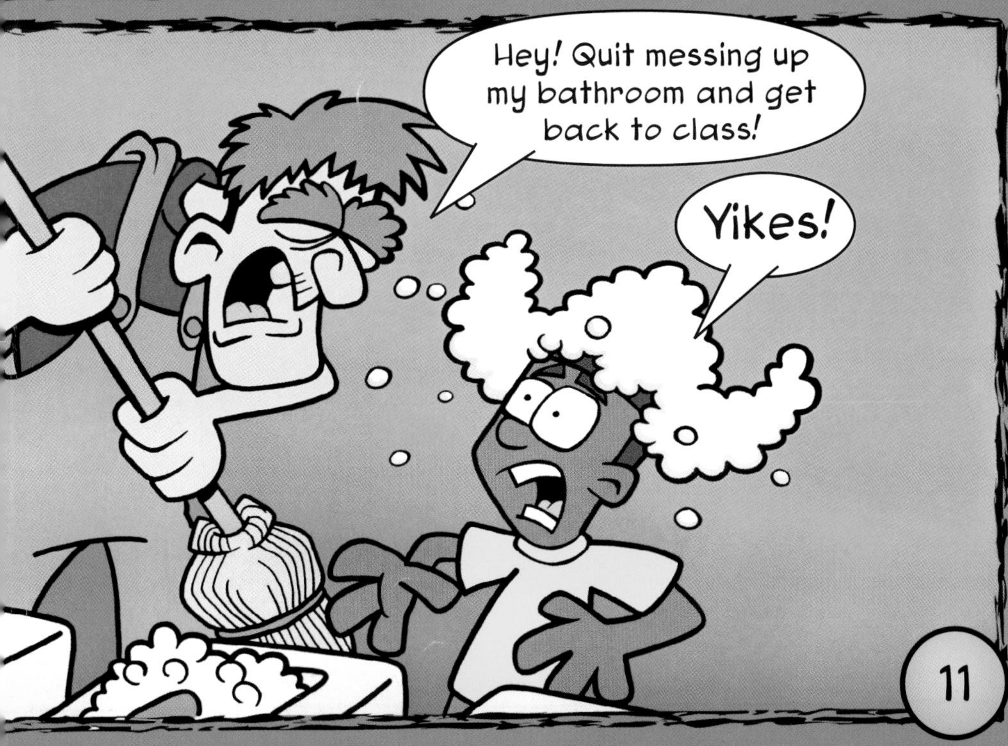
Hey! Quit messing up my bathroom and get back to class!
Yikes!

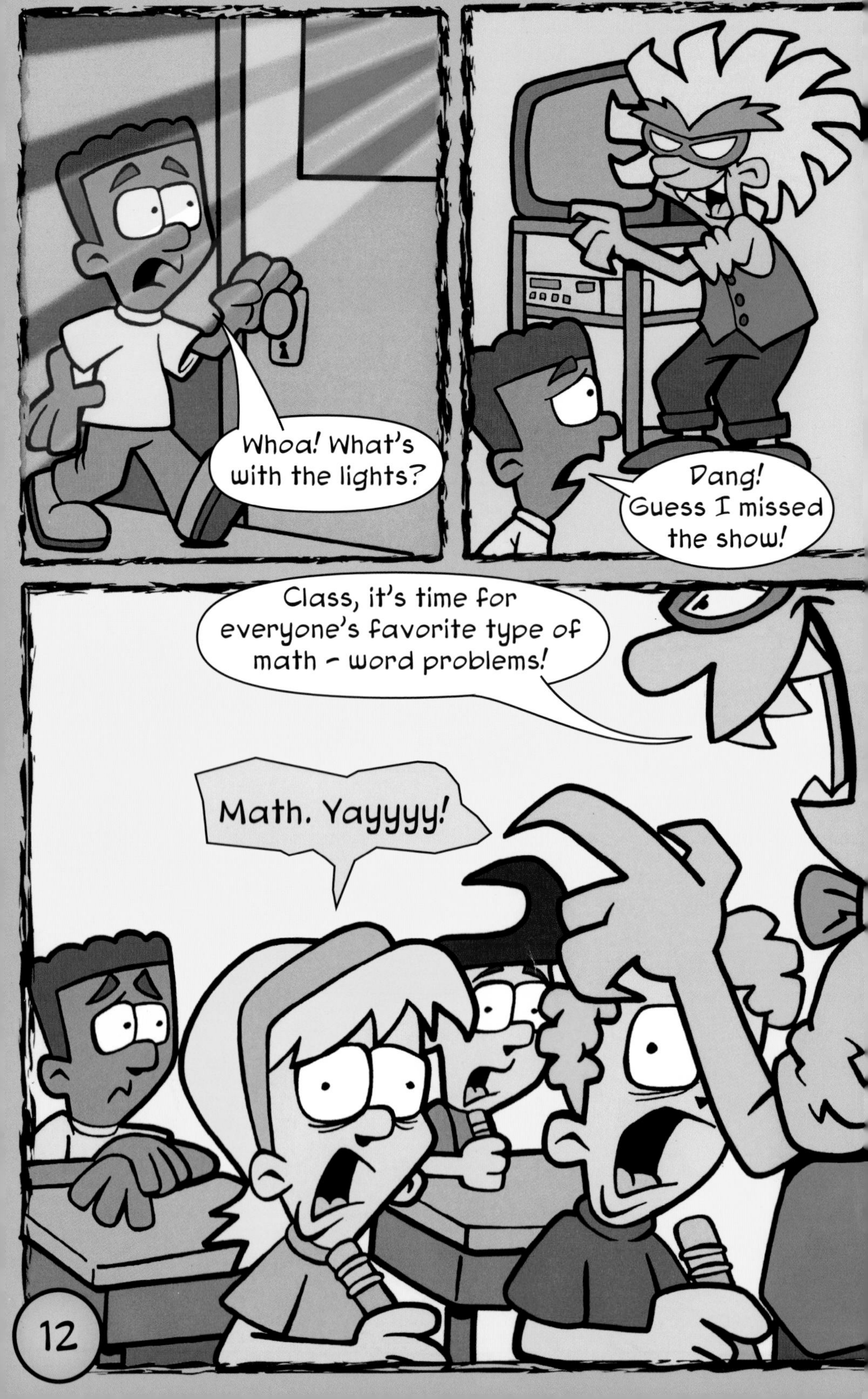

Whoa! What's with the lights?
Dang! Guess I missed the show!
Class, it's time for everyone's favorite type of math - word problems!
Math. Yayyyy!

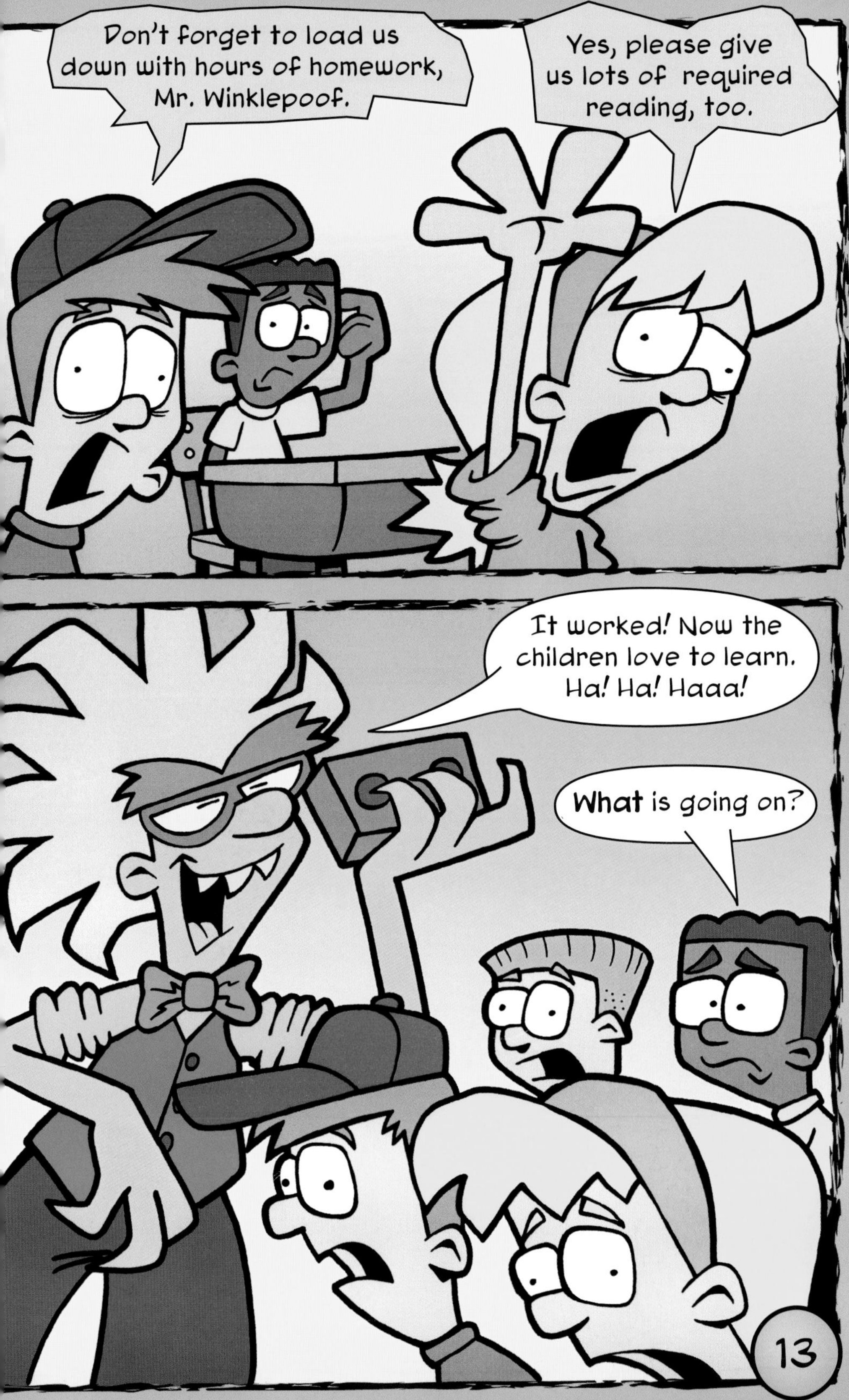
Don't forget to load us down with hours of homework, Mr. Winklepoof.
Yes, please give us lots of required reading, too.
It worked! Now the children love to learn. Ha! Ha! Haaa!
What is going on?

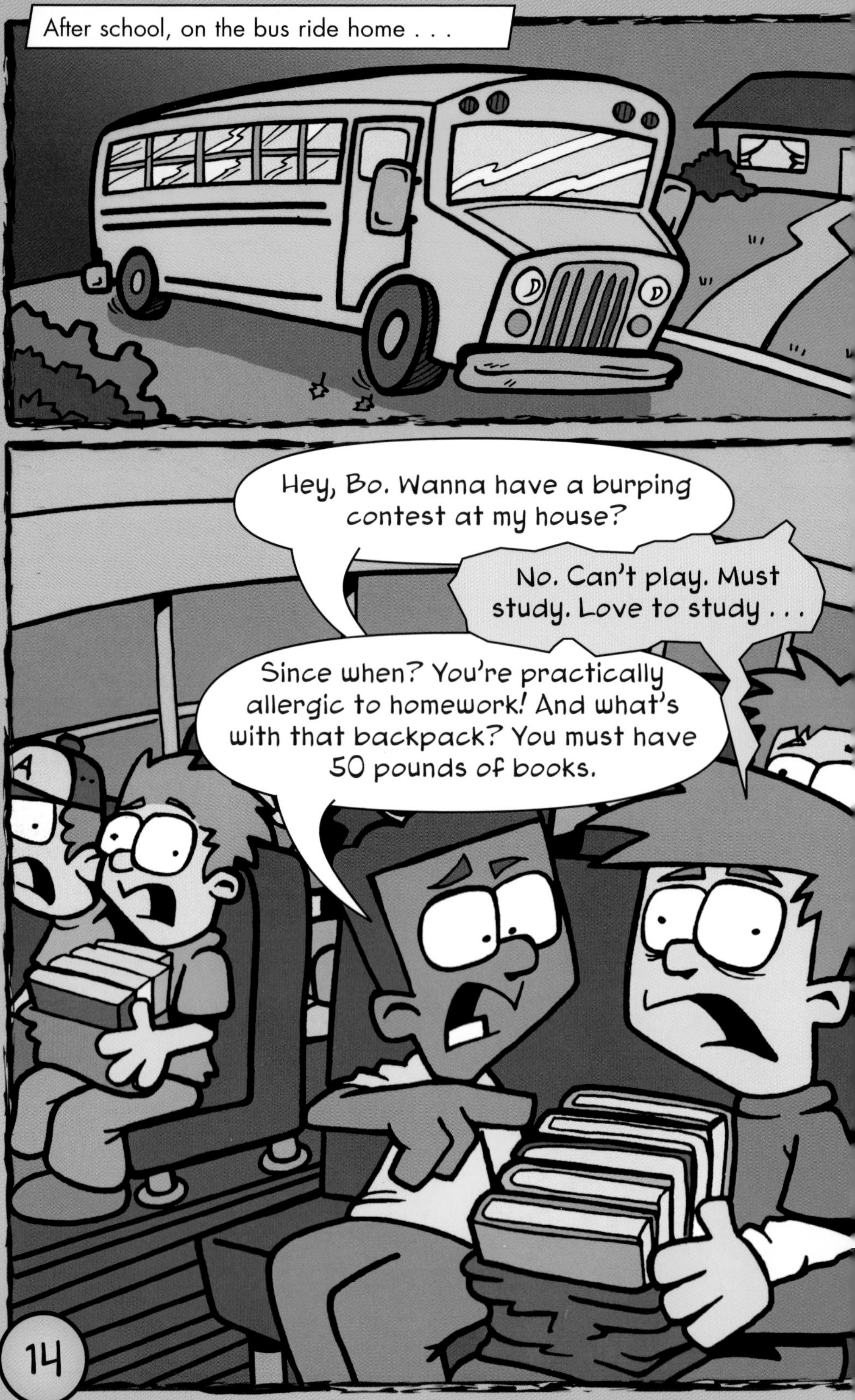
After school, on the bus ride home . . .
Hey, Bo. Wanna have a burping contest at my house?
No. Can't play. Must study. Love to study . . .
Since when? You're practically allergic to homework! And what's with that backpack? You must have 50 pounds of books.

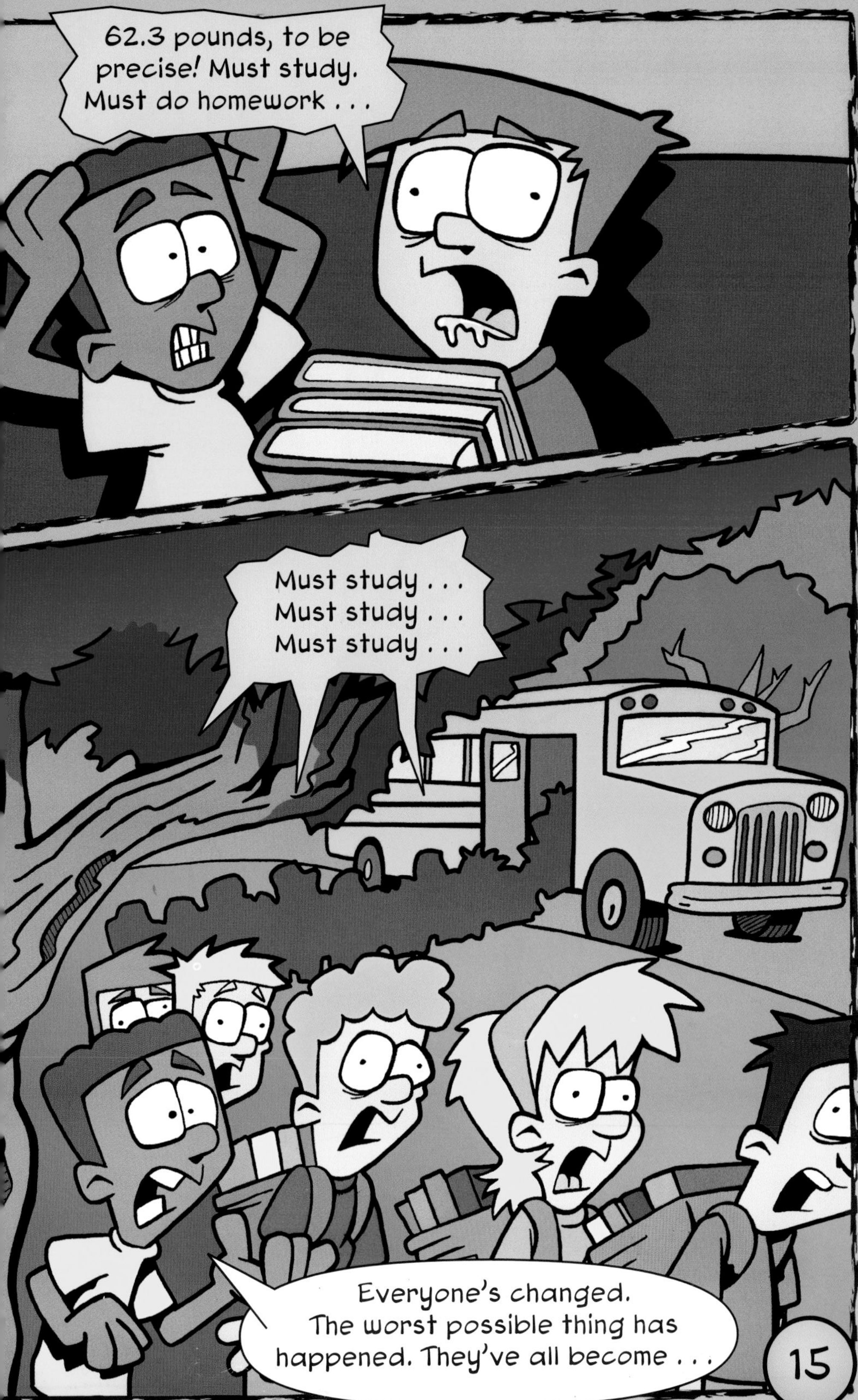
62.3 pounds, to be precise! Must study. Must do homework . . .
Must study . . . Must study . . . Must study . . .
Everyone's changed. The worst possible thing has happened. They've all become . . .

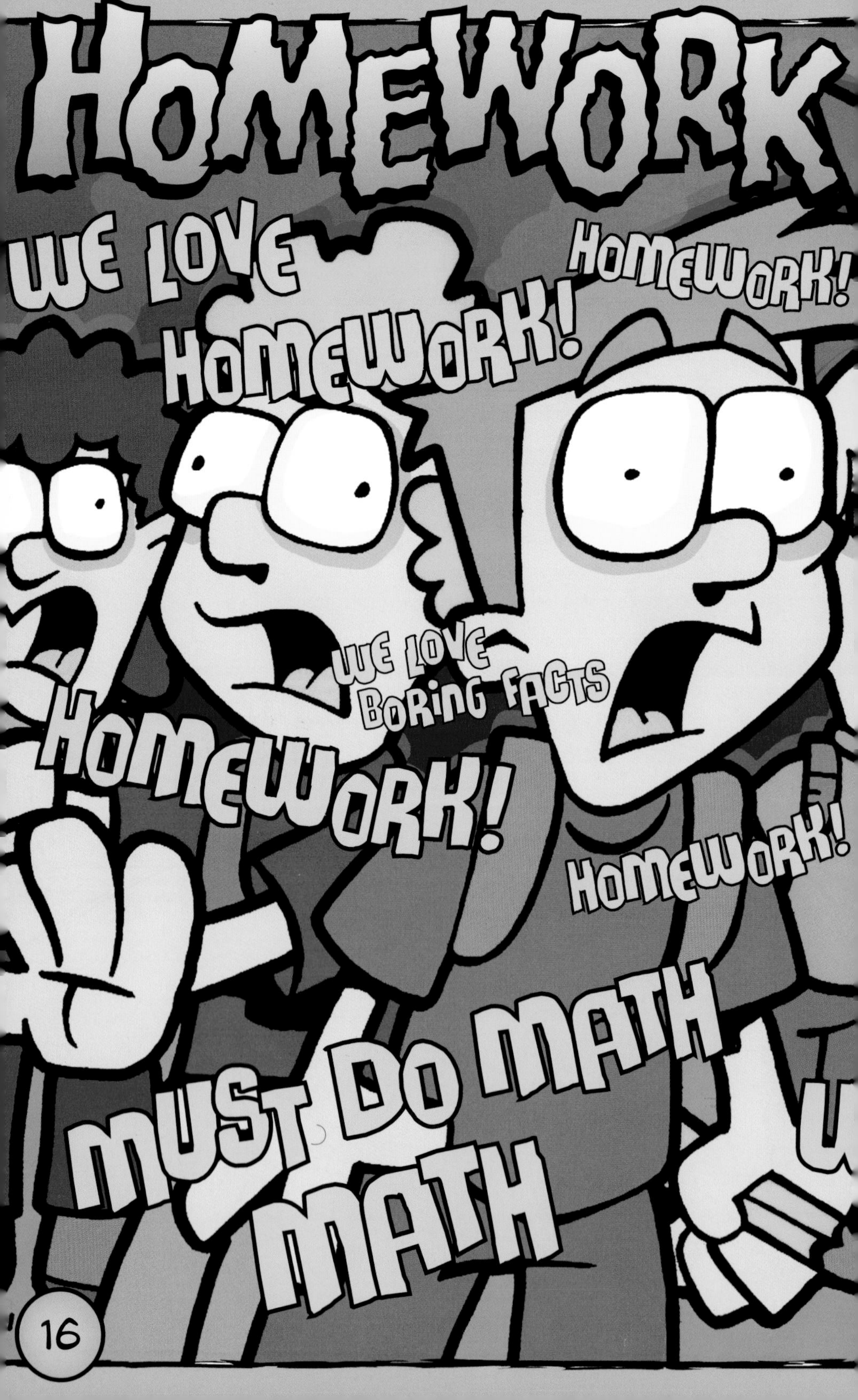
HOMEWORK
WE LOVE HOMEWORK!
HOMEWORK!
WE LOVE BORING FACTS
HOMEWORK!
HOMEWORK!
MUST DO MATH
MATH

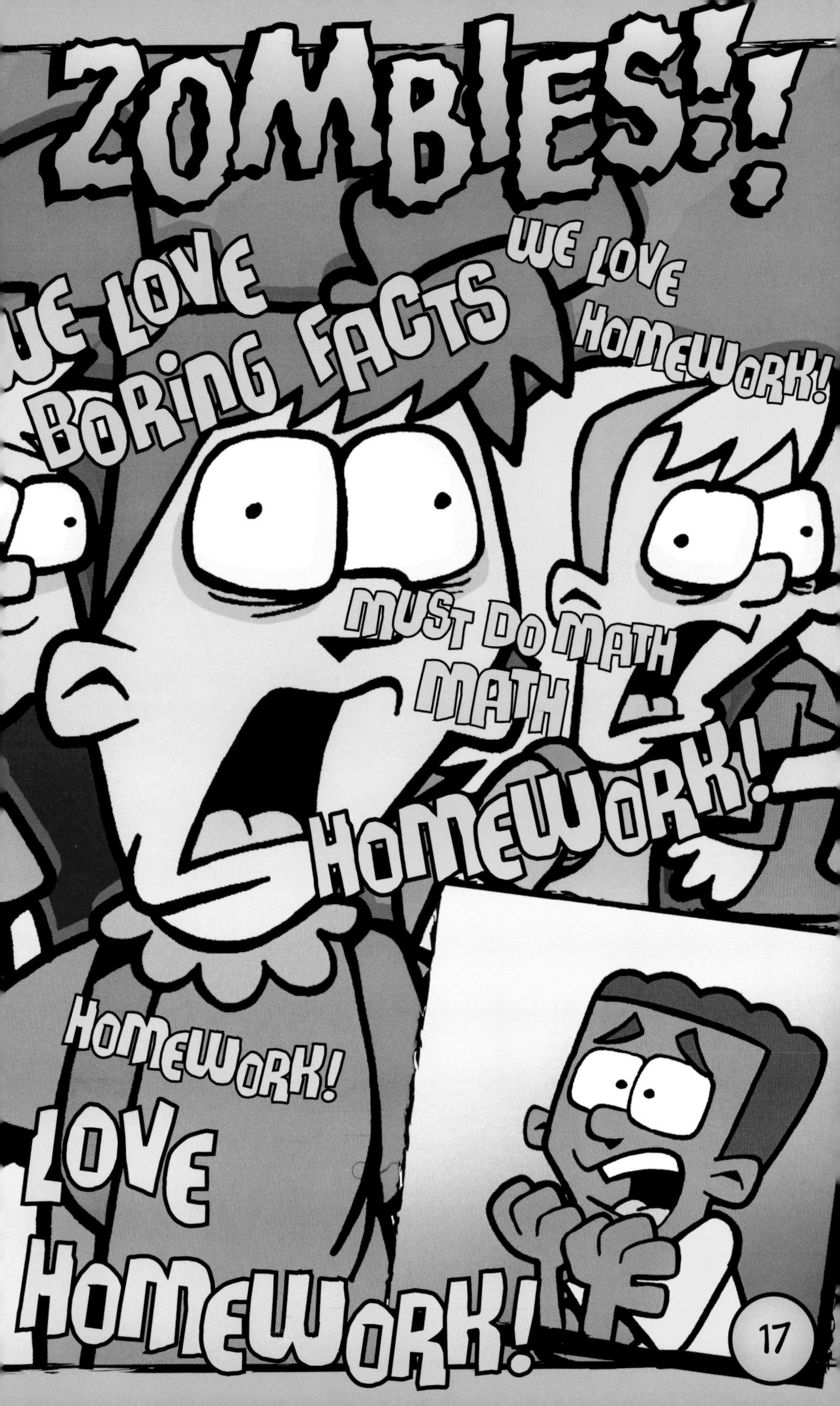

ZOMBIES!!
WE LOVE BORING FACTS
WE LOVE HOMEWORK!
MUST DO MATH MATH
HOMEWORK!
HOMEWORK!
LOVE HOMEWORK!

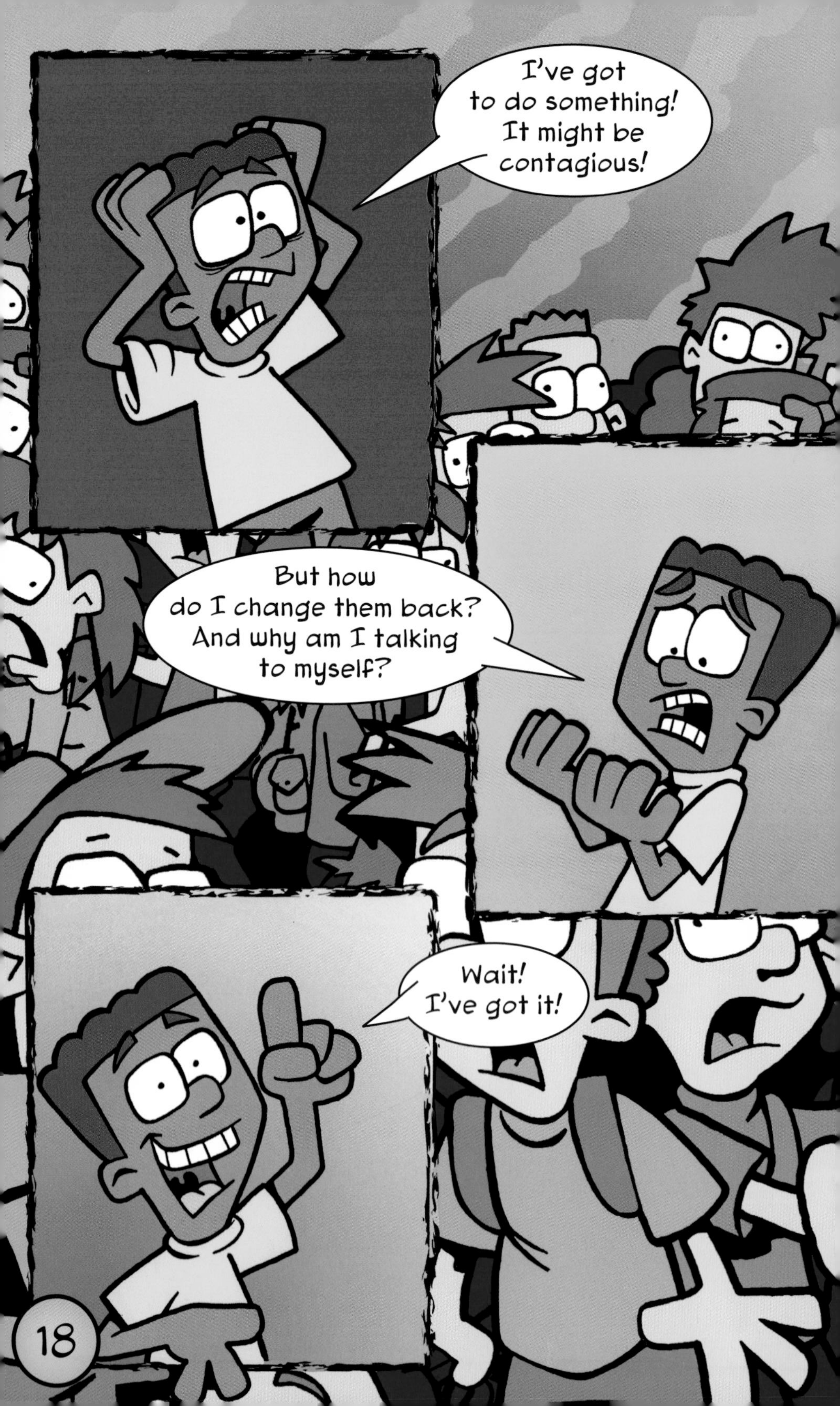

I've got to do something! It might be contagious!
But how do I change them back? And why am I talking to myself?
Wait! I've got it!

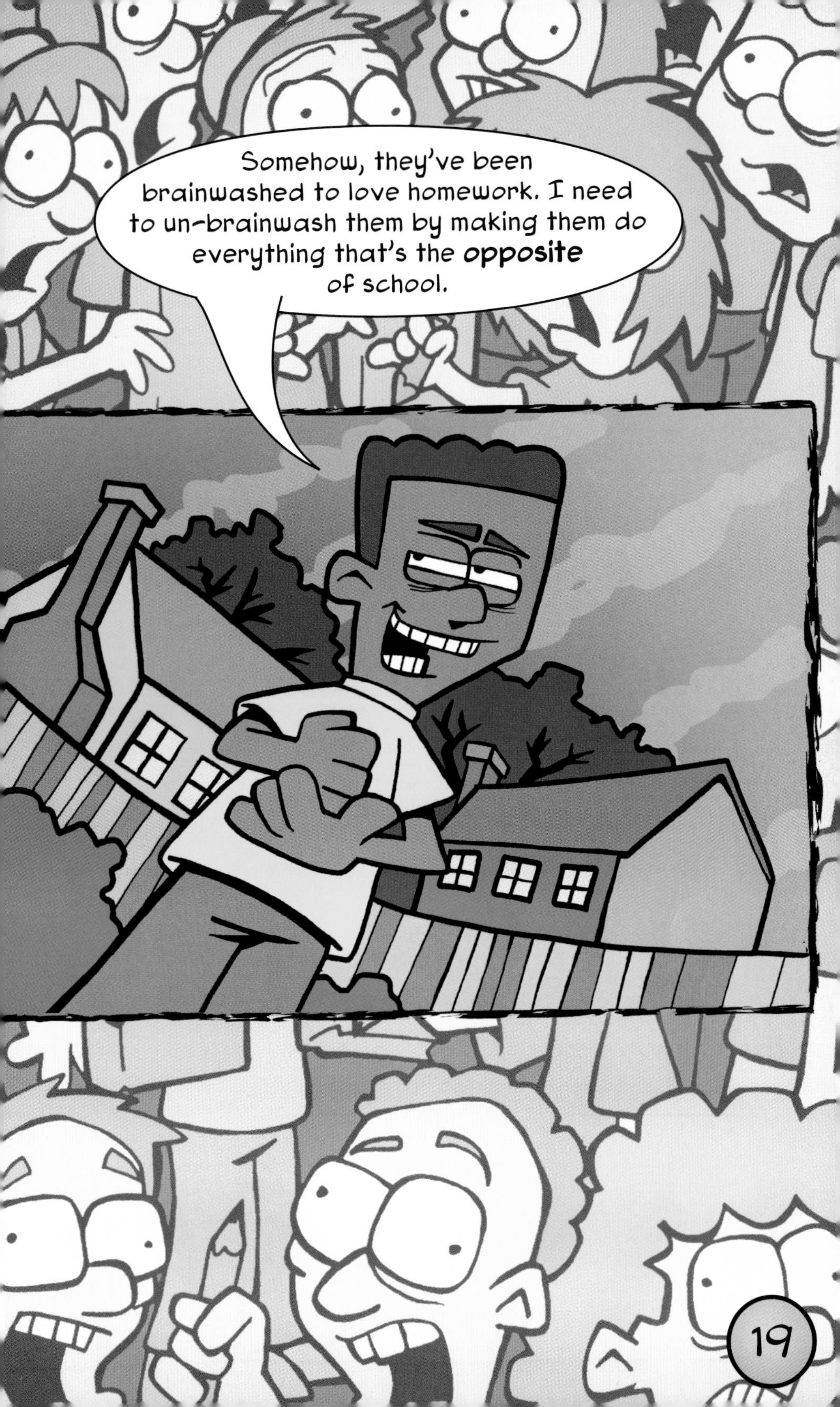
Somehow, they've been brainwashed to love homework. I need to un-brainwash them by making them do everything that's the **opposite** of school.

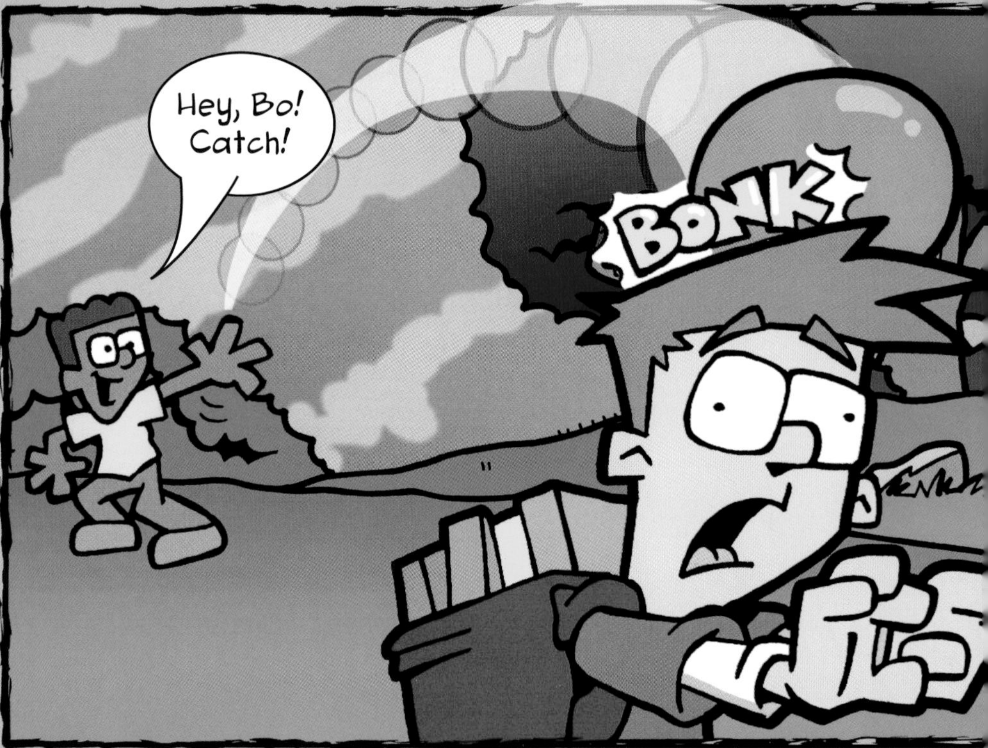
Hey, Bo!
Catch!
BONK

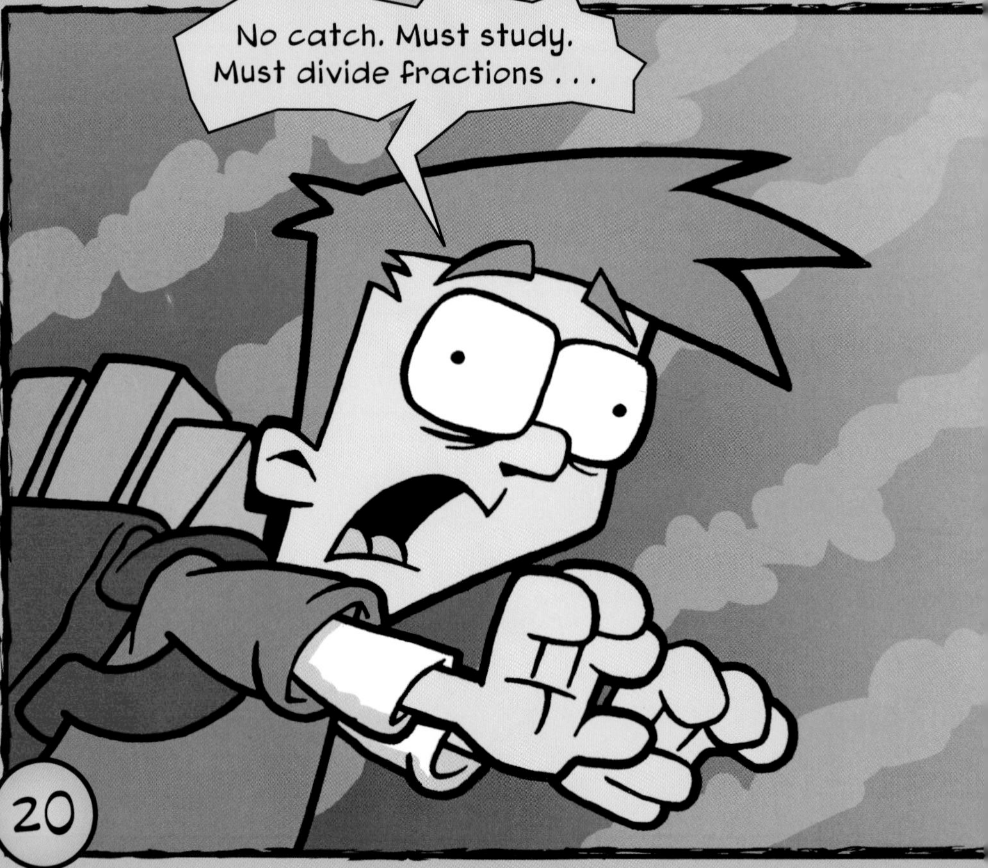
No catch. Must study.
Must divide fractions . . .

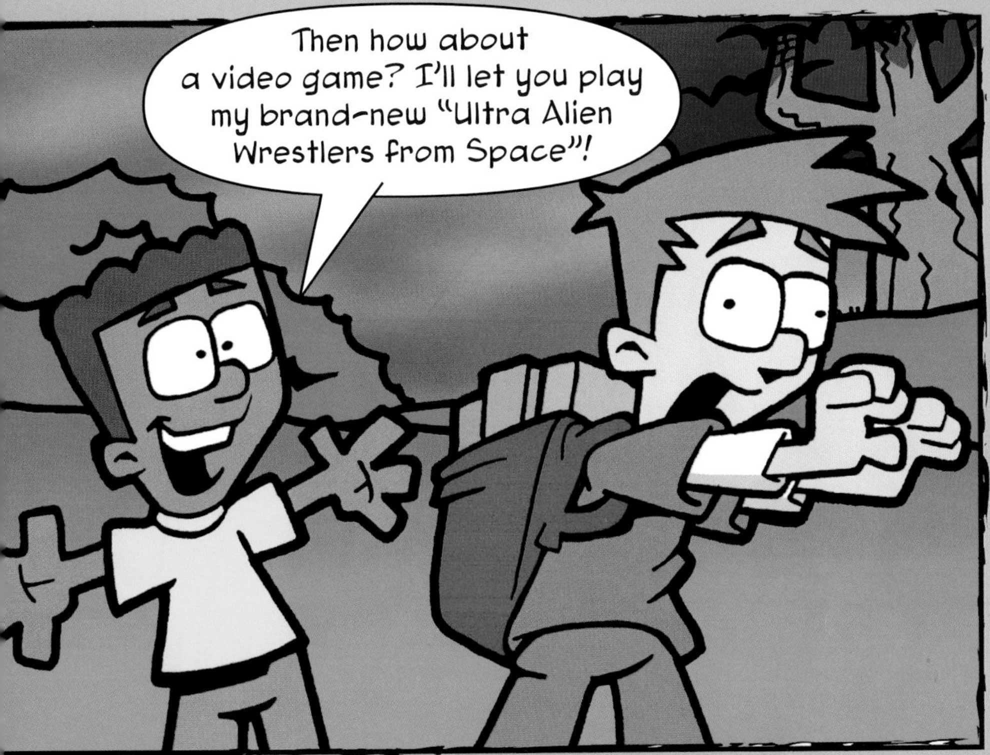
Then how about a video game? I'll let you play my brand-new "Ultra Alien Wrestlers from Space"!

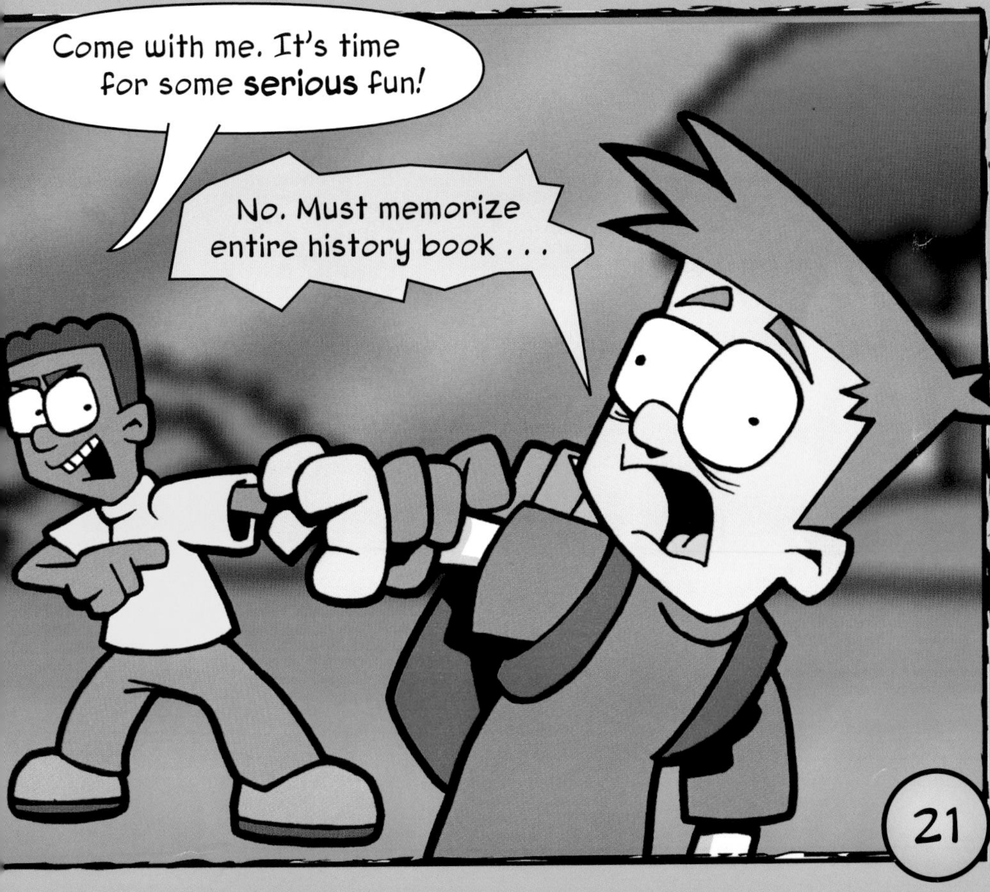
Come with me. It's time for some **serious** fun!
No. Must memorize entire history book . . .

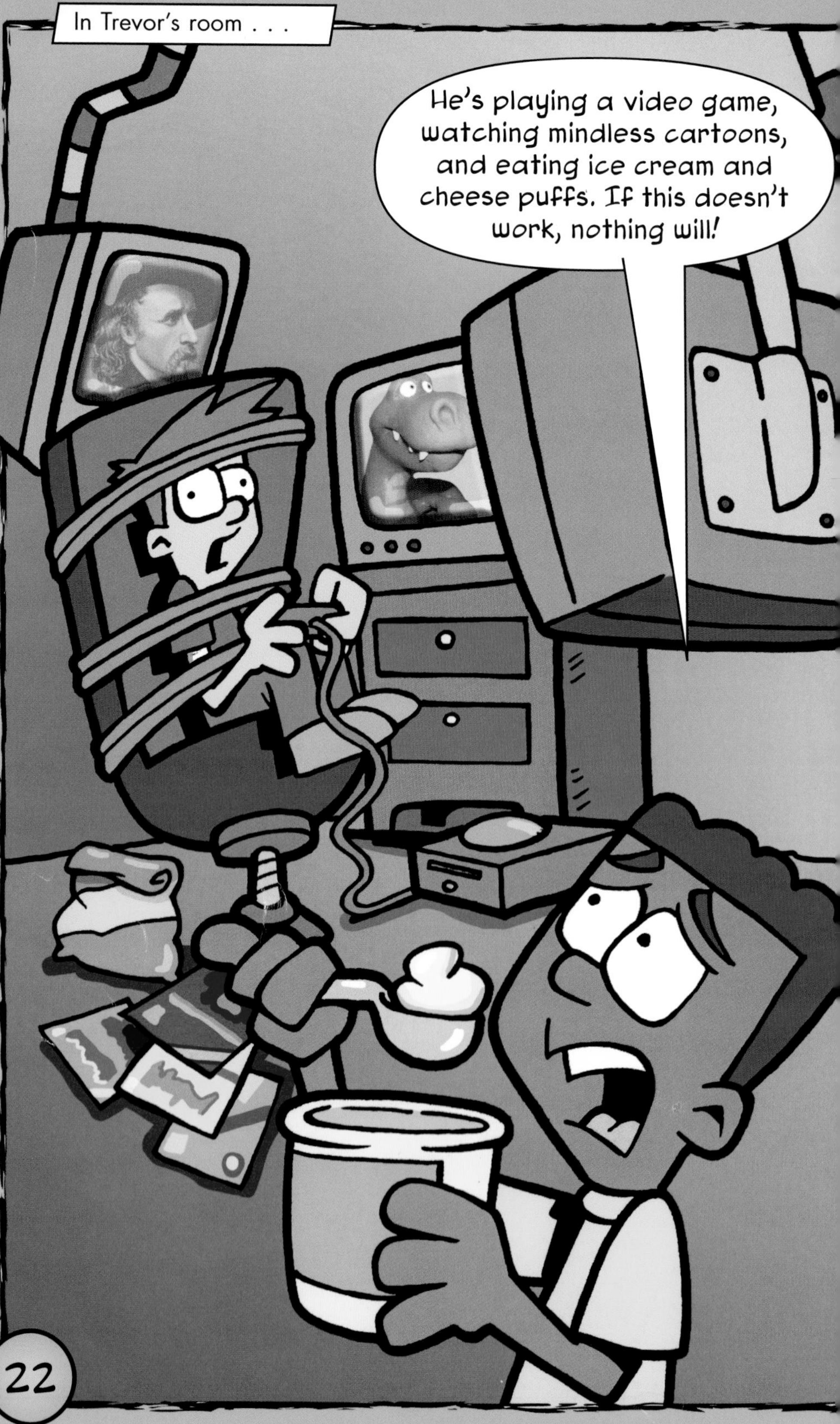
In Trevor's room . . .
He's playing a video game, watching mindless cartoons, and eating ice cream and cheese puffs. If this doesn't work, nothing will!

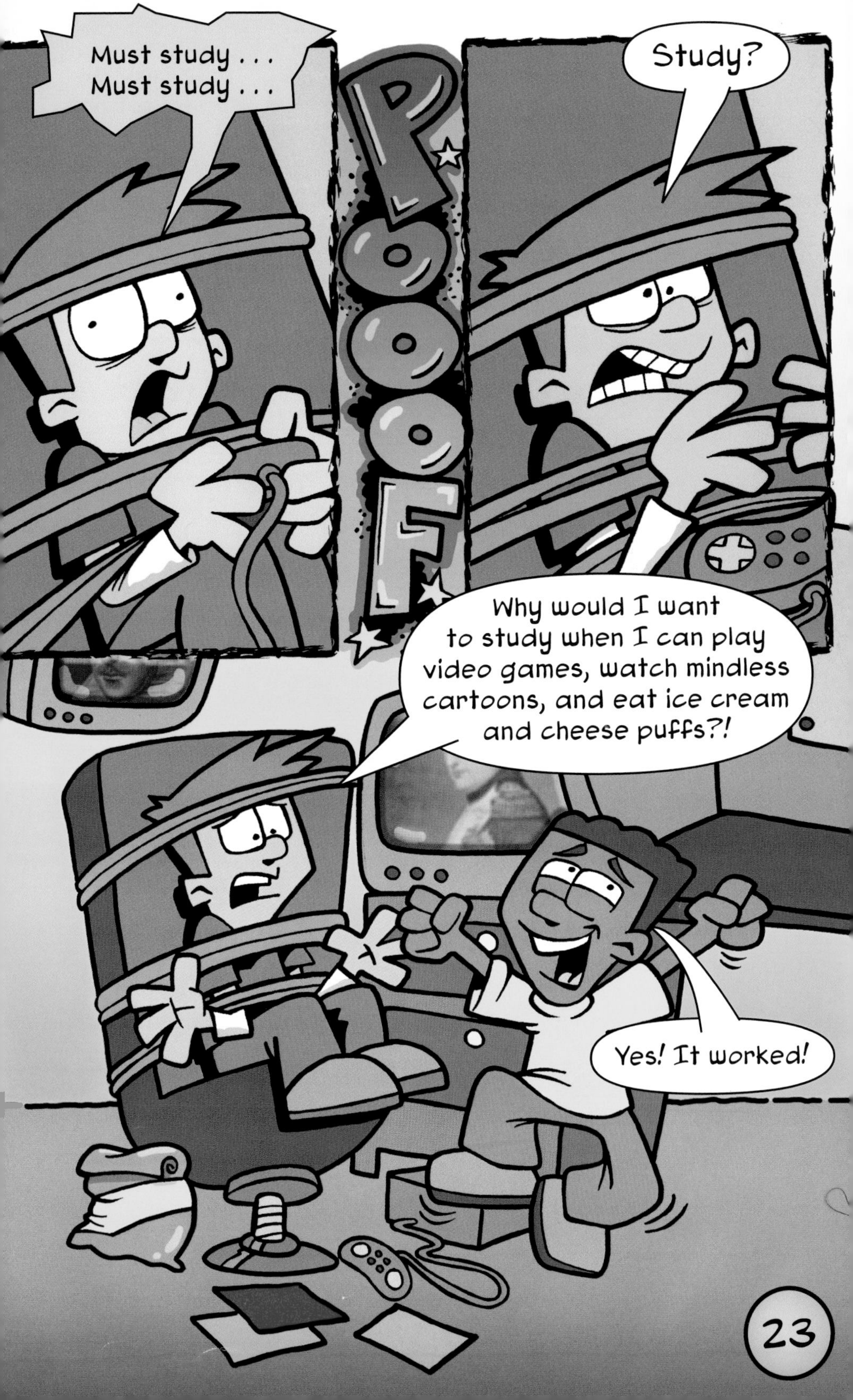
Must study . . .
Must study . . .
POOF
Study?
Why would I want to study when I can play video games, watch mindless cartoons, and eat ice cream and cheese puffs?!
Yes! It worked!

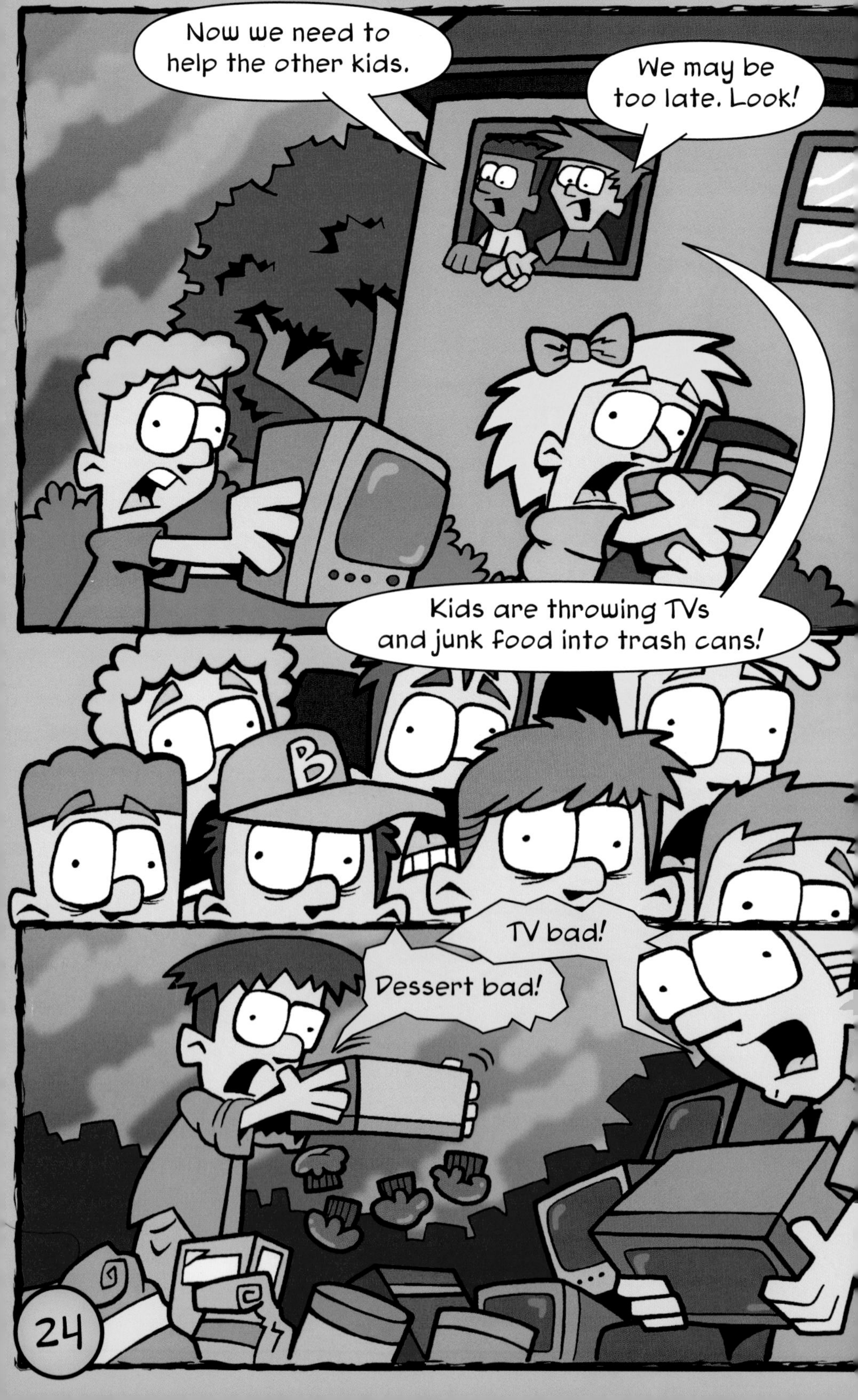
Now we need to help the other kids.
We may be too late. Look!
Kids are throwing TVs and junk food into trash cans!
TV bad!
Dessert bad!

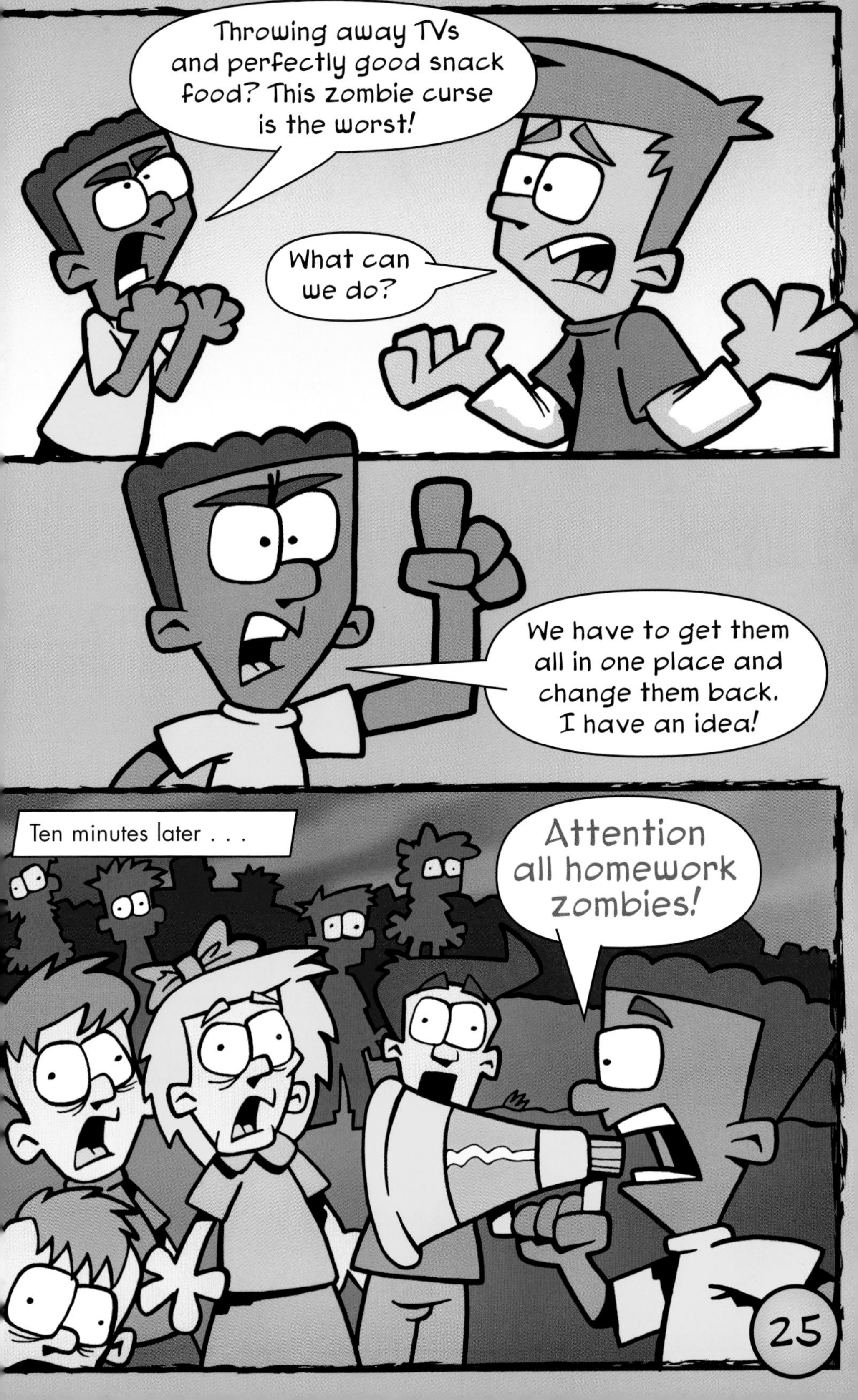
Throwing away TVs and perfectly good snack food? This zombie curse is the worst!
What can we do?
We have to get them all in one place and change them back. I have an idea!
Ten minutes later . . .
Attention all homework zombies!

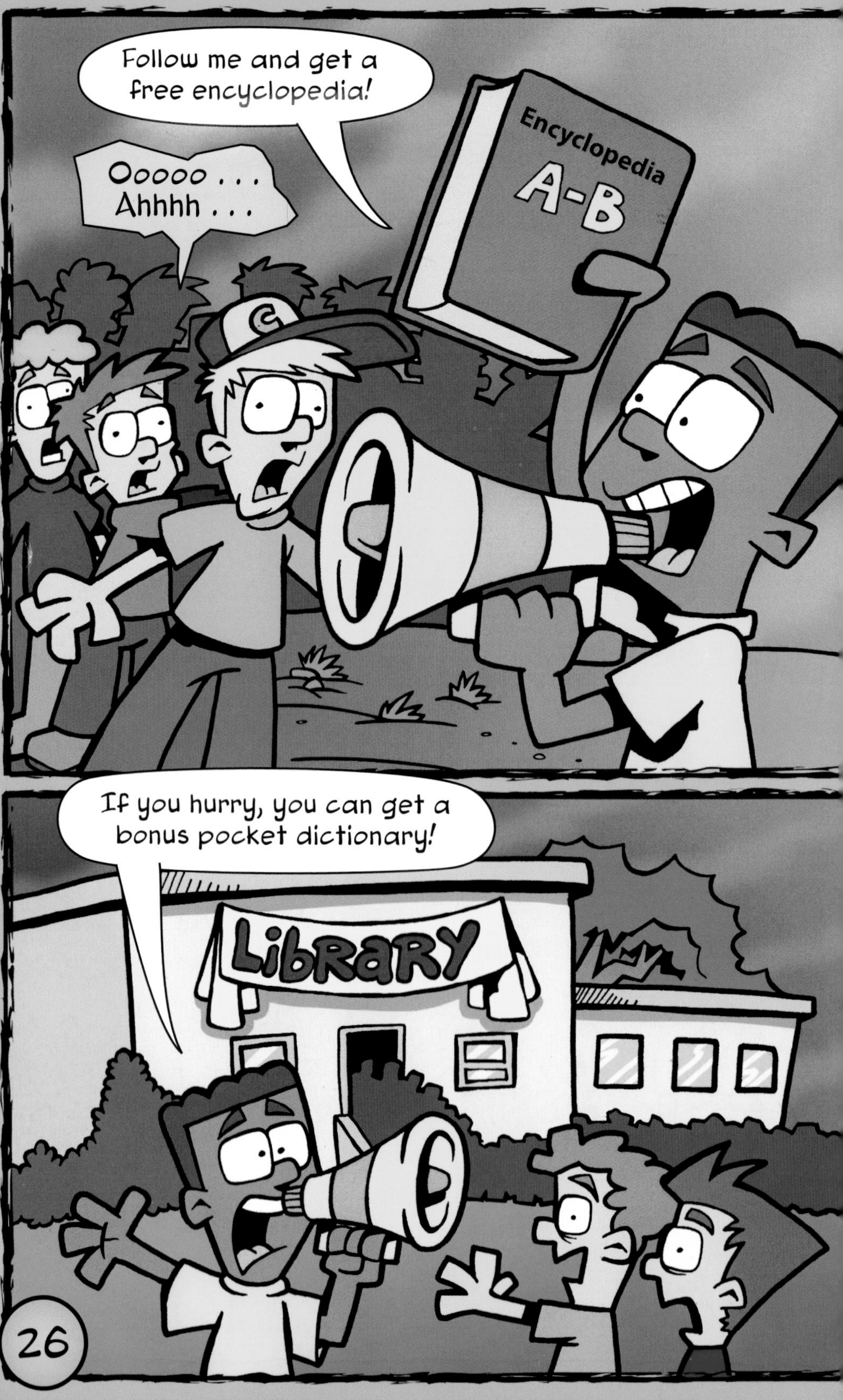
Follow me and get a free encyclopedia!
Ooooo . . . Ahhhh . . .
Encyclopedia A-B
If you hurry, you can get a bonus pocket dictionary!
LIBRARY

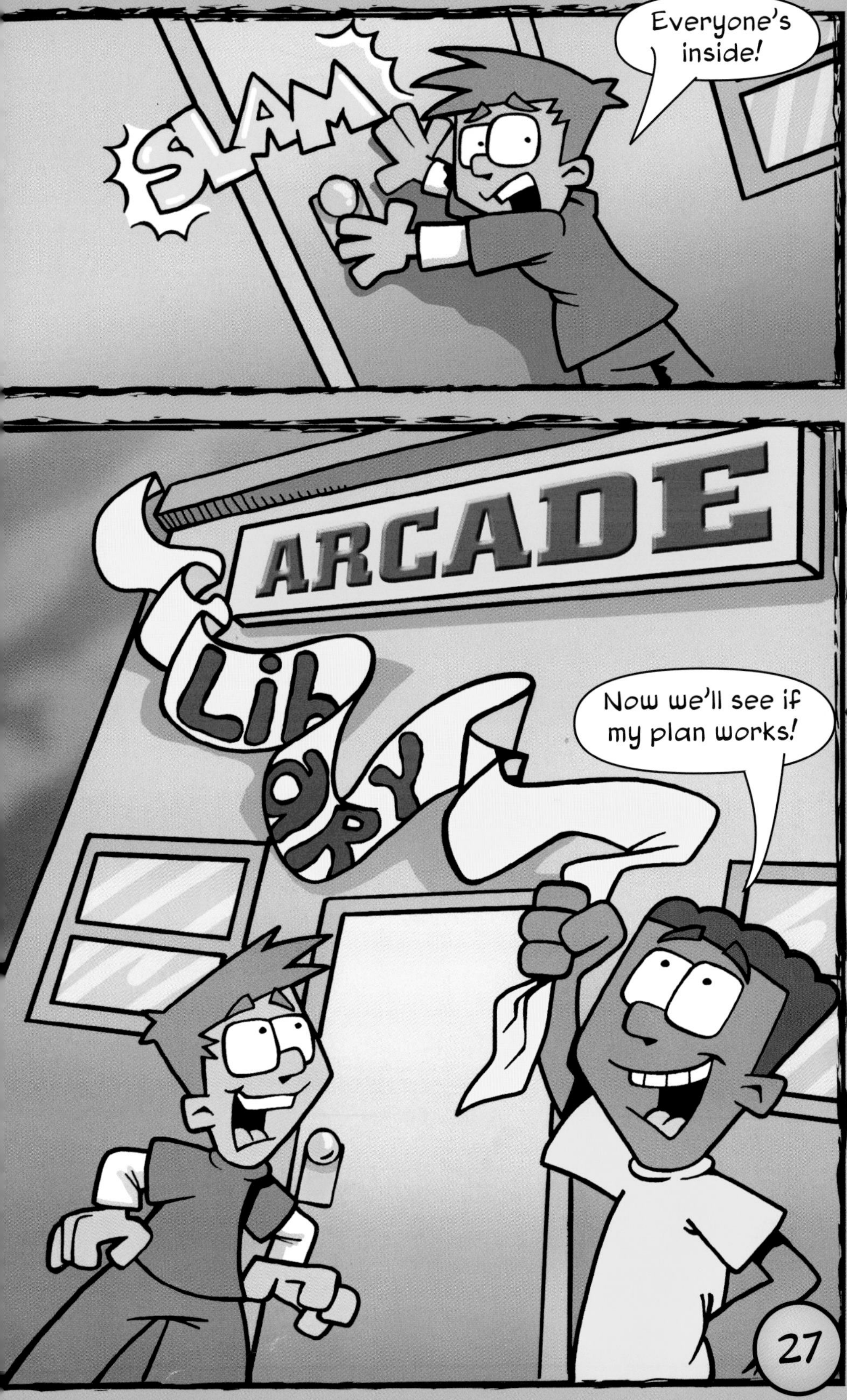
SLAM
Everyone's inside!
ARCADE
Library
Now we'll see if my plan works!

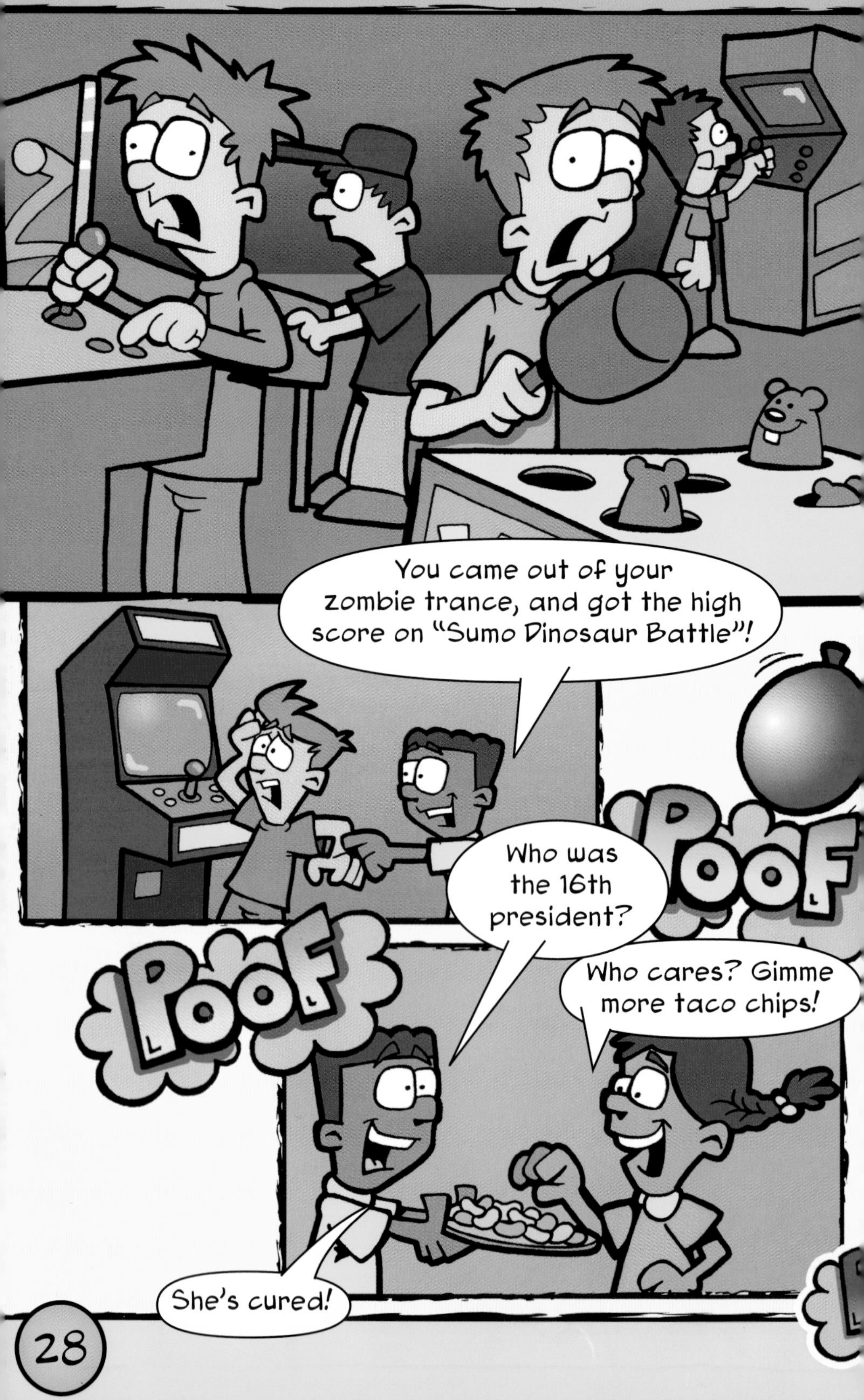

You came out of your zombie trance, and got the high score on "Sumo Dinosaur Battle"!
POOF
Who was the 16th president?
POOF
Who cares? Gimme more taco chips!
She's cured!

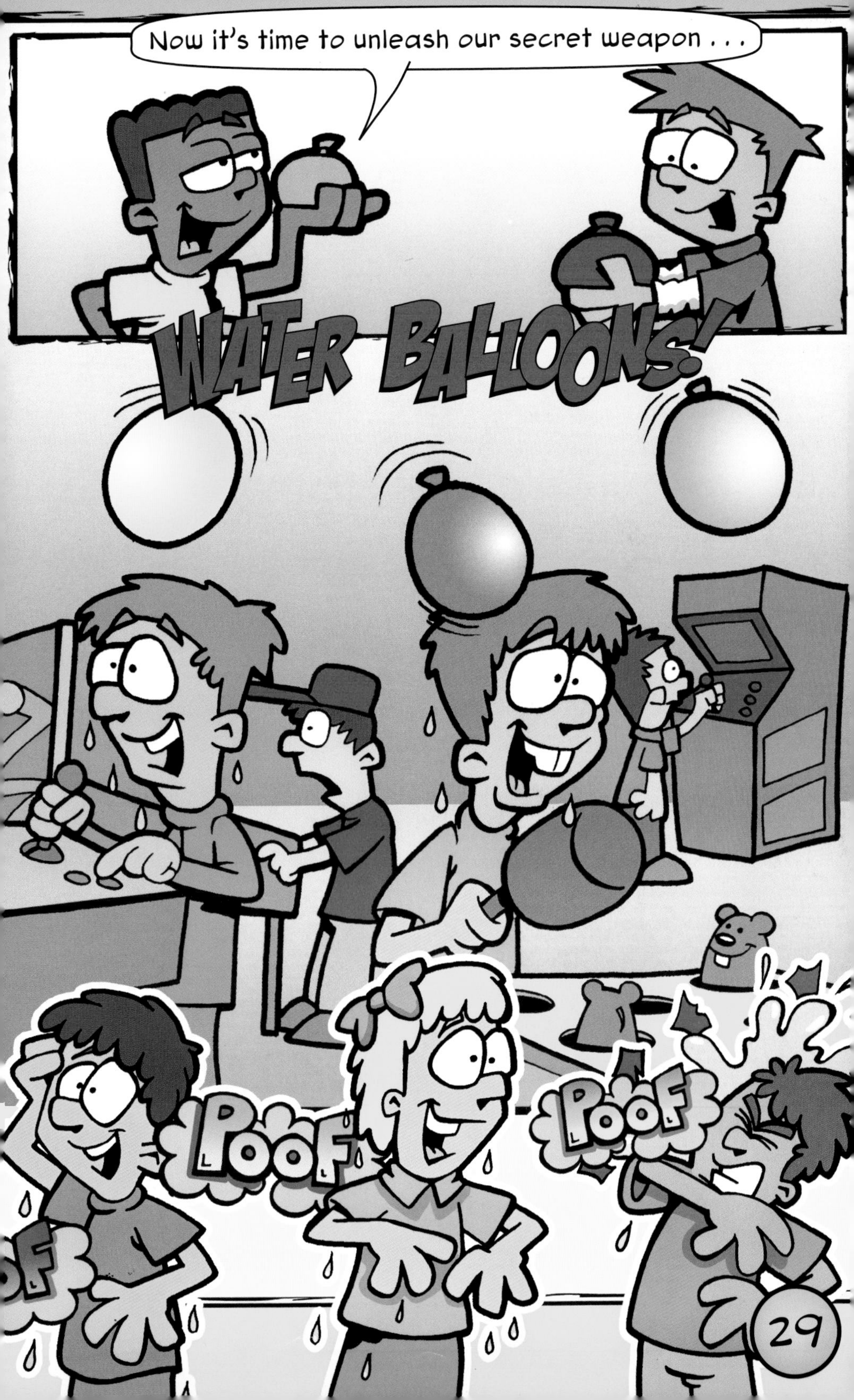
Now it's time to unleash our secret weapon . . .
WATER BALLOONS!
POOF
POOF
POOF

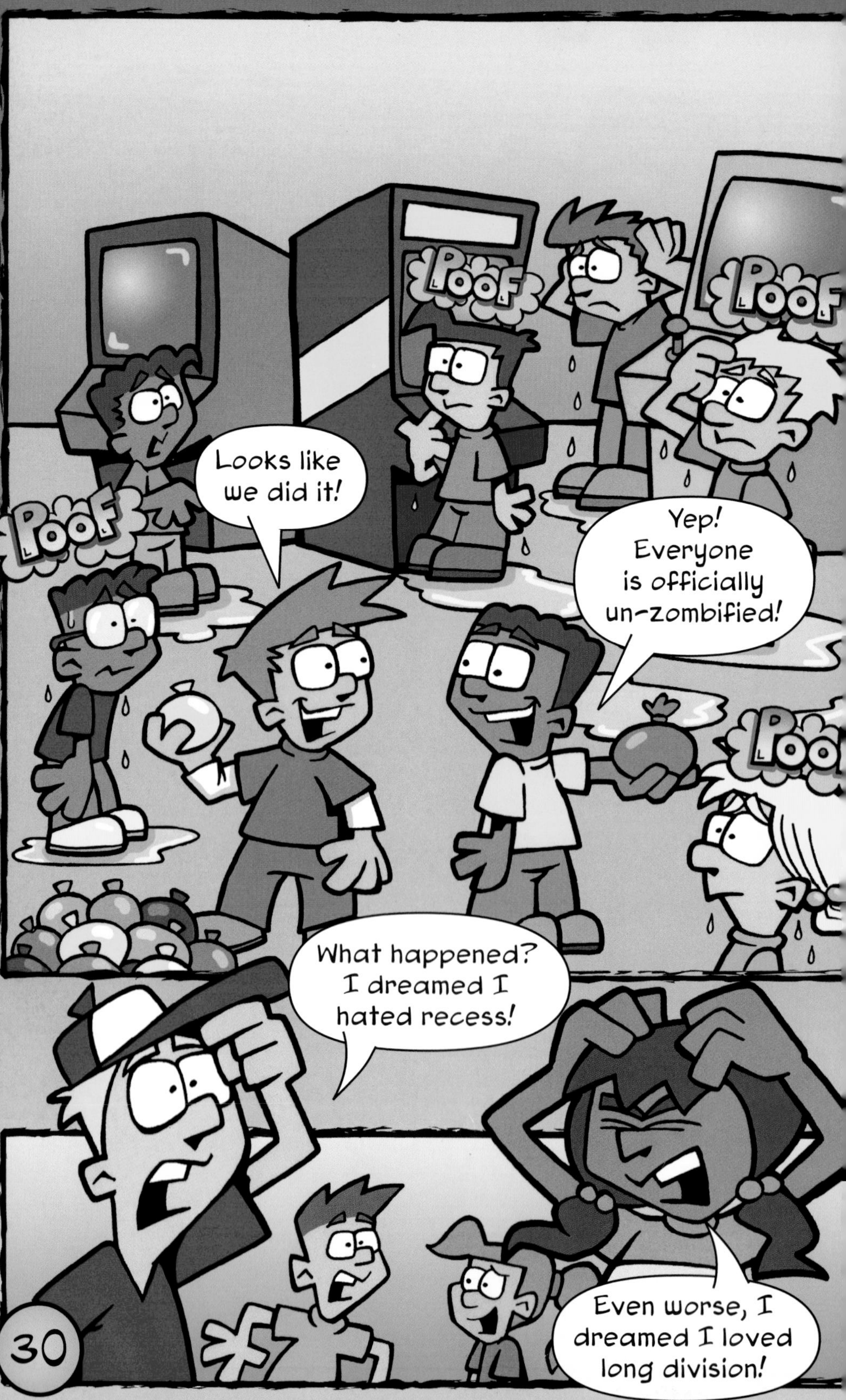
POOF
POOF
Looks like we did it!
POOF
Yep! Everyone is officially un-zombified!
POOF
What happened? I dreamed I hated recess!
Even worse, I dreamed I loved long division!

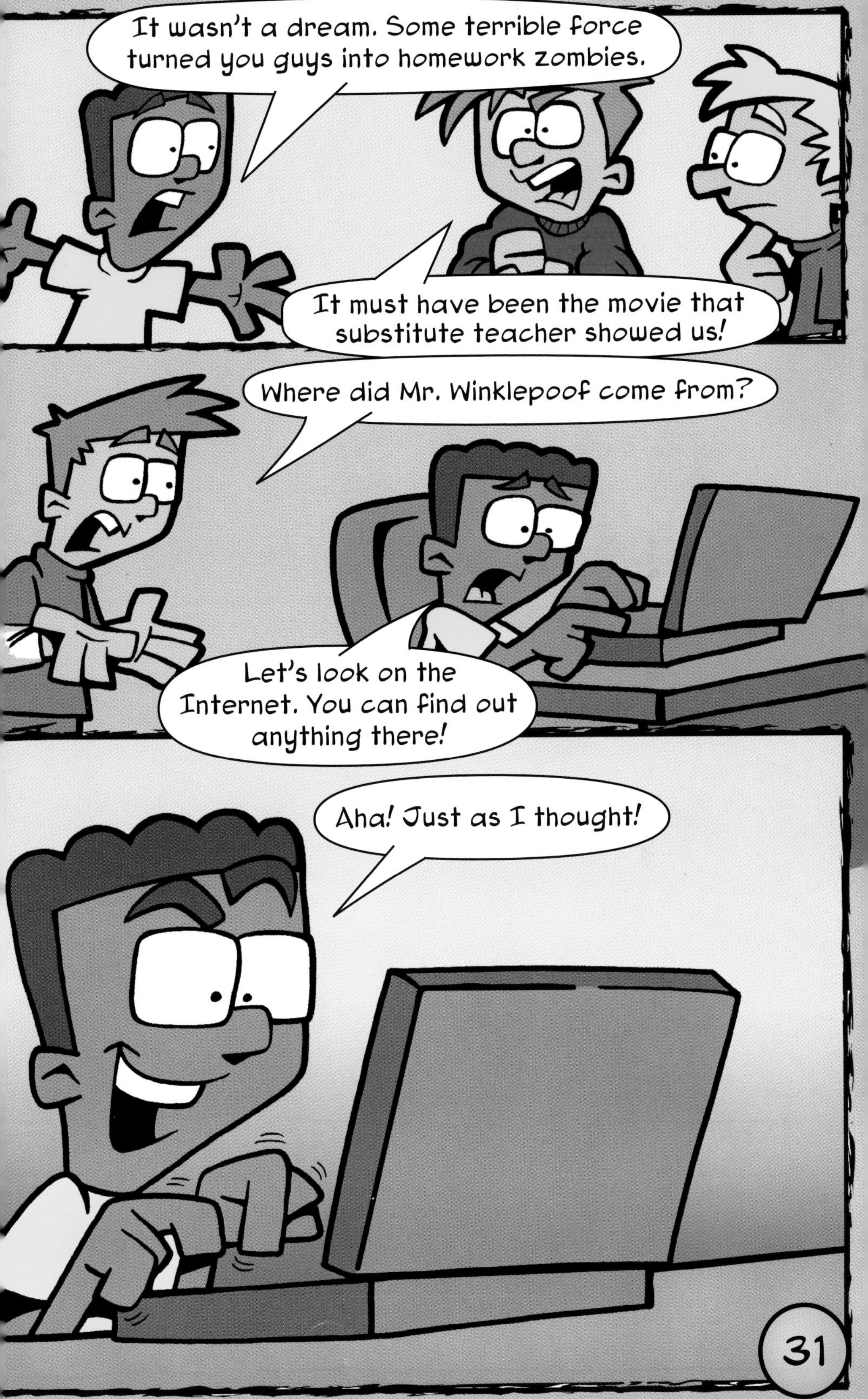
It wasn't a dream. Some terrible force turned you guys into homework zombies.
It must have been the movie that substitute teacher showed us!
Where did Mr. Winklepoof come from?
Let's look on the Internet. You can find out anything there!
Aha! Just as I thought!

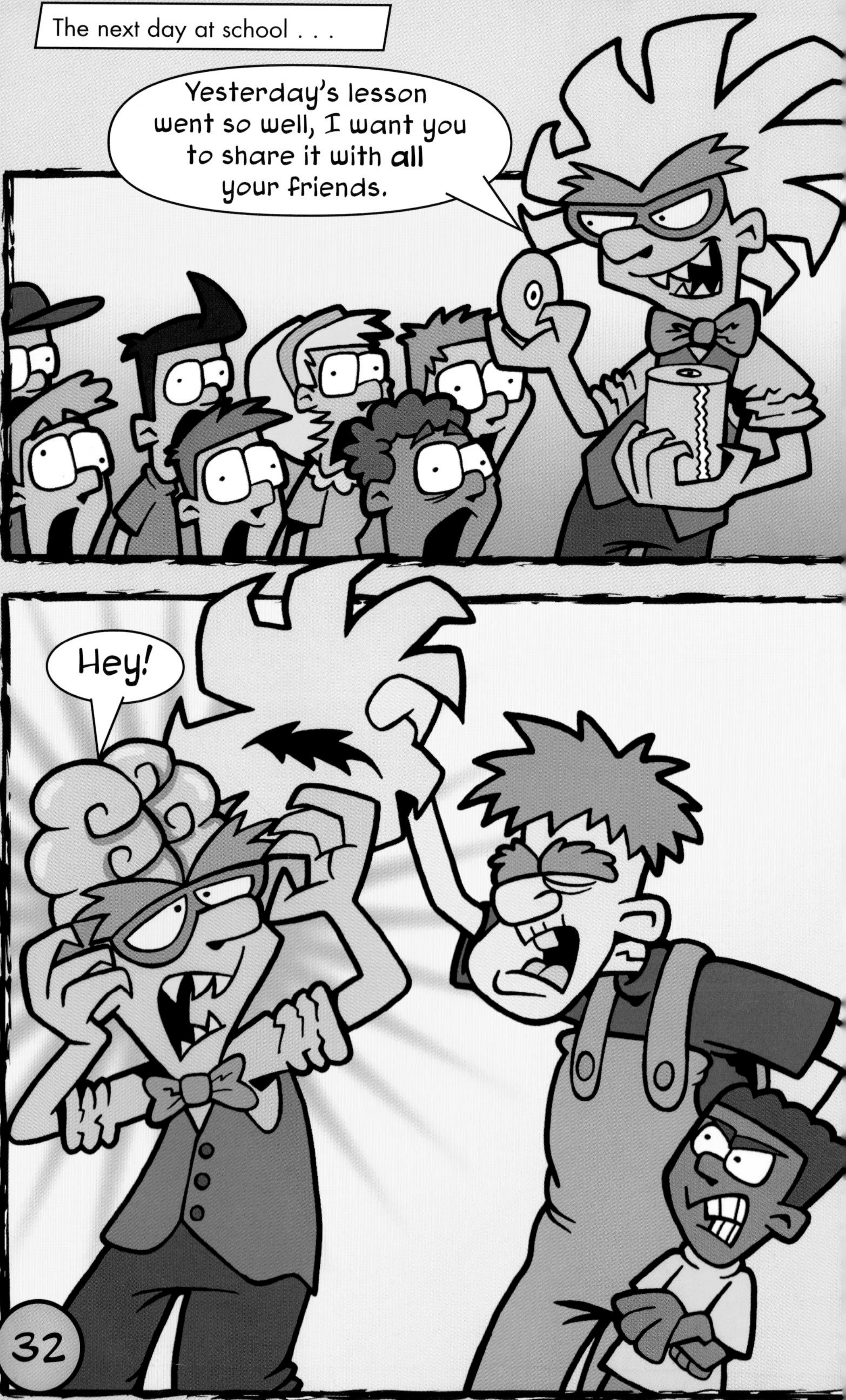

The next day at school . . .
Yesterday's lesson went so well, I want you to share it with all your friends.
Hey!

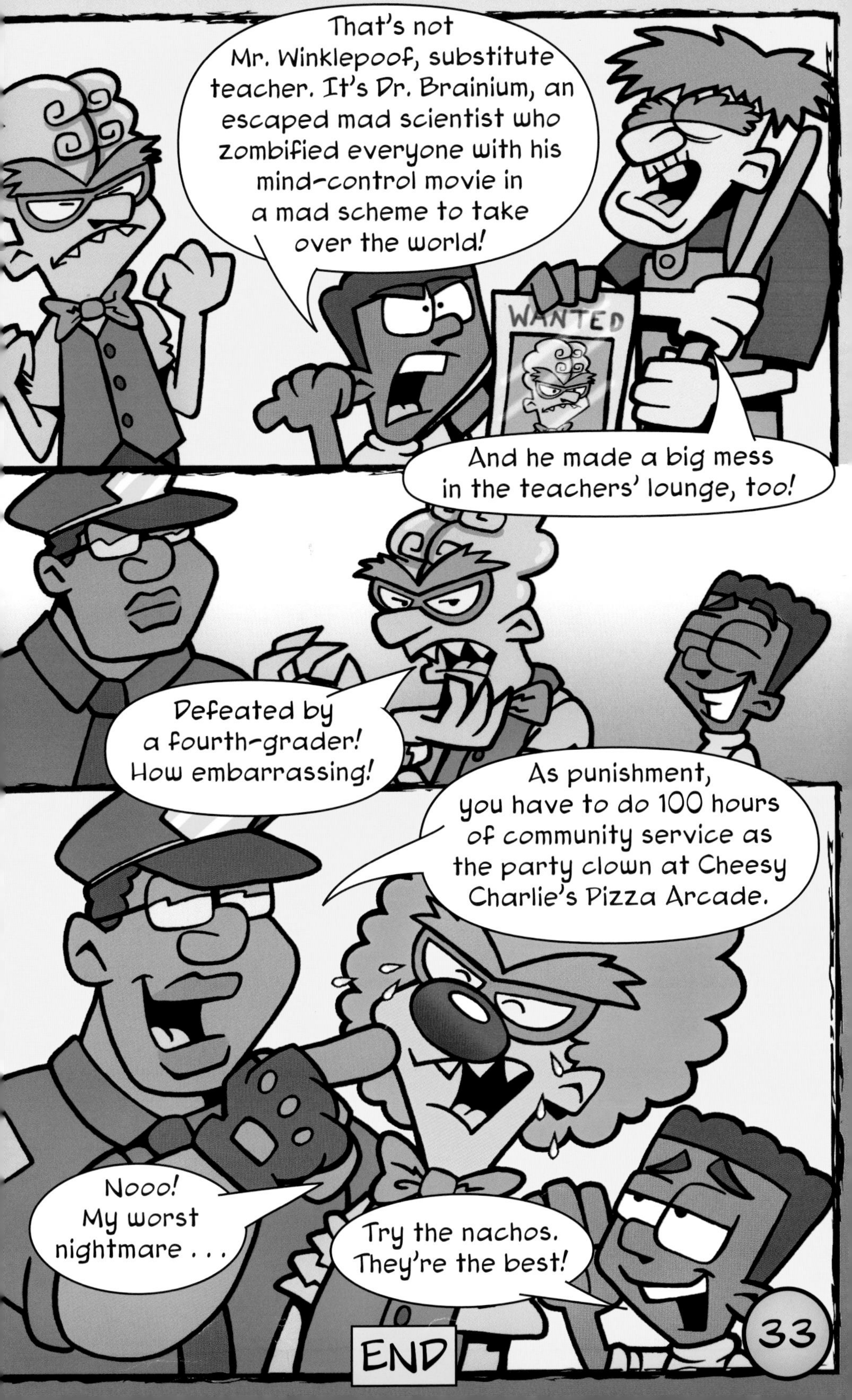
That's not Mr. Winklepoof, substitute teacher. It's Dr. Brainium, an escaped mad scientist who zombified everyone with his mind-control movie in a mad scheme to take over the world!
WANTED
And he made a big mess in the teachers' lounge, too!
Defeated by a fourth-grader! How embarrassing!
As punishment, you have to do 100 hours of community service as the party clown at Cheesy Charlie's Pizza Arcade.
Nooo! My worst nightmare . . .
Try the nachos. They're the best!
END

ABOUT THE AUTHOR

Scott Nickel has written children's books, short fiction for *Boys' Life Magazine*, humorous greeting cards, and lots of really funny knock-knock jokes. Scott is also the author of many Garfield books.

Currently, Scott lives in Indiana with his wife, two sons, four cats, a parakeet, and several sea monkeys.

ABOUT THE ILLUSTRATOR

Steve Harpster has loved to draw funny cartoons, mean monsters, and goofy gadgets since he was able to pick up a pencil. In first grade, he was able to avoid his writing assignments by working on the pictures for stories instead.

Steve was able to land a job drawing funny pictures for books, and that's really what he's best at. Steve lives in Columbus, Ohio, with his wonderful wife, Karen, and their sheepdog, Doodle.

GLOSSARY

brainwash (BRAYN-wash) to make people act, or think, in a new way without them knowing it; the brain is "washed clean" of its old way of thinking.

contagious (kun-TAY-juhss) something that can spread from one person to another; a sickness can be contagious, or becoming a zombie, but boy-germs and girl-germs are not contagious.

mindless (MYND-liss) an activity is mindless if you don't have to use your brain while you're doing it; watching TV is mindless, but reading a graphic novel is not!

substitute (SUHB-stuh-toot) someone who takes another person's place, such as a substitute teacher or a substitute quarterback in a football game

zombie (ZOM-bee) someone whose brain is controlled by another person; when you tell your friend to eat worms, and he does it, he is acting like a zombie

zombify (ZOM-buh-fye) to turn someone into a zombie

Heh-heh-heh. If you learn these words your brain will get bigger. And BIGGER!!

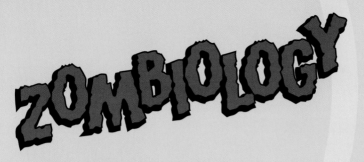

ZOMBIOLOGY

Are zombies real?

Some people think so. On the islands of the Caribbean, some people practice a religion known as Voudon, or voodoo. Voodoo beliefs say that a dead body can come back to life. A spirit, called a zombi, enters the dead body and gives it the power to move.

Zombie!
Zombie!
I want to be
a zombie!

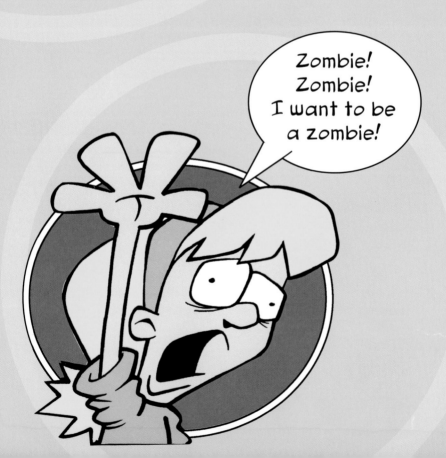

What does a zombie look like?

Zombies do not eat or drink. They move stiffly, have blank faces, and cannot speak. Real people who act like this, maybe a grown-up after a hard day at the office, are sometimes called zombies.

According to voodoo, zombies are under the control of the person who brought them back to life. Some scientists think that people given powerful drugs can behave like zombies. The drugs weaken their minds so that they will easily obey another person.

Computers can also be zombies. A zombie computer is one that is remotely controlled by another person in secret.

The famous writer Zora Neale Hurston met people on the island of Haiti who claimed to have seen a real zombie. A woman who had been buried 30 years earlier was walking the streets of a village. Later, Hurston found out that this was just a rumor.

DISCUSSION QUESTIONS

1.) Dr. Brainium brainwashes students so they will love homework. Homework is supposed to be good for you. So is it all right to be brainwashed into doing it?

2.) Trevor uses his own brainpower to come up with a plan to defeat Dr. Brainium. Who do you think is smarter, and why?

3.) Bo is saved from Dr. Brainium's evil scheme by his best friend Trevor. Trevor had to force Bo into watching cartoons and eating ice cream and cheese puffs. Is Trevor just as guilty of brainwashing as Dr. Brainium?

WRITING PROMPTS

1.) If you were Doctor Brainium and could brainwash other people into obeying your commands, what would you make them do, and why?

2.) Trevor is the only kid who escapes the brainwashing video because he was wasting time in the boys' bathroom. Write a story about what would happen if Trevor had stayed in the classroom along with everyone else. Would the students stay brainwashed forever?

3.) At the end of the story, the evil scientist is punished by having to work at Cheesy Charlie's Pizza Arcade. Write a story about what might happen if you went to a pizza place and met a mad scientist.

INTERNET

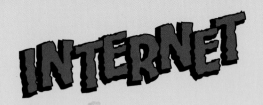

Do you want to know more about subjects related to this book? Or are you interested in learning about other topics? Then check out FactHound, a fun, easy way to find Internet sites.

Our investigative staff has already sniffed out great sites for you!

Here's how to use FactHound:

1.) Visit *www.facthound.com*

2.) Select your grade level.

3.) To learn more about subjects related to this book, type in the book's ISBN number: **1598890352**. If you're looking for information on another subject, simply type in a keyword.

4.) Click the **Fetch It** button.

FactHound will fetch the best Internet sites for you.

WWW.FACTHOUND.COM℠

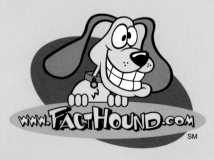